Anne Thackeray Ritchie

Da Capo

And other Tales

Anne Thackeray Ritchie

Da Capo
And other Tales

ISBN/EAN: 9783337082505

Printed in Europe, USA, Canada, Australia, Japan

Cover: Foto ©Andreas Hilbeck / pixelio.de

More available books at **www.hansebooks.com**

DA CAPO

AND OTHER TALES

BY

MISS THACKERAY,

AUTHOR OF "THE STORY OF ELIZABETH," ETC.

COPYRIGHT EDITION.

LEIPZIG

BERNHARD TAUCHNITZ

1880.

CONTENTS.

DA CAPO.

CHAPTER I.

COLONEL BAXTER'S RETROSPECTIONS.

It is a curious experience to come back in after years to an old mood and to find it all changed and swept and garnished; emotionless, orderly now;—are the devils of indifference and selfish preoccupation those against which we are warned in the parable? Perhaps it is some old once-read and re-read letter which has brought it all back to you; perhaps it is some person quietly walking in, followed by a whole train of associations. Who has not answered to the call of an old tune breaking the dream of to-day? Is the past, past, if such trifles can recall it all vividly again, or only not-present?

One day Colonel Baxter, an officer lately returned from abroad, came up to the door of an old house in Sussex, and stopped for an instant before he

rang the bell. The not-present suddenly swept away
all the fabric of the last few years. He stopped,
looking for a little phantom of five years before that
he could still conjure up, coming flitting along the
terrace, gentle, capricious, lovely Felicia Marlow, as
he remembered her at eighteen, and not so happy
as eighteen should be. The little phantom had once
appealed to him for help, and it had needed all
Colonel Baxter's years of service, all his standing in
the army, all the courage of a self-reliant man, and
all the energies of his Victoria Cross and many
clasps to help him to withstand the innocent entreaty
of those two wild grey eyes which had said "Help
me, help me!" The story was simple enough, and
one which has been told before, of a foolish little
creature who had scarcely been beyond the iron
scrolls of the gates of Harpington Court, who had
been promised to her cousin, the only man she had
ever seen, and who suddenly finding a world beyond
her own, had realised the possibility of a love that
was not her cousin James's old familiar everyday,
ever-since-she-could-remember, mood.

Colonel Baxter had seen the world and travelled
far beyond Harpington, but nevertheless he, too,
had been carried away by the touching vehemence
of this poor little victim to circumstances, and felt
that he could give his whole life to make her more

happy. Only somehow it was not for him to make her happy. That right then belonged to James Marlow, who was Baxter's friend, and one of the best and most loyal of men.

Baxter walked up to the gates and stopped to look round, as I have said, before he rang. The place was changed. A new spirit seemed to have come over the periwinkle avenue. There were bright flowers in tubs at intervals along the road; a couple of gardeners were at work in the sunshine, chipping, chopping, binding up all the drifts and wreaths, carefully nipping away all ·the desolate sweetness and carrying it off in wheelbarrows. Gay striped blinds were sprouting from the old diamond windows; Minton china twinkled on the terrace; the stone steps had been repaired and smartened up somehow; a green trellis had been nailed against the walls. It was scarcely possible to see in which of these trifling signs the difference lay, but it was unmistakable. Once more an old feeling seemed to come over the man as he tramped along the gravel walks with long even strides; a feeling of hopeless separation, of utter and insurmountable distance: all this orderly comfort seemed to come only to divide them. In the old days of her forlorn negligence and trouble Felicia had seemed nearer, far nearer than now. When he had come back after James's death,

he had thought it wrong to obtrude his personal
feelings. He was then under orders to rejoin his
regiment. Before he went to India, he had written
an ambiguous little message to Felicia Marlow, to
which no answer had come; he had been too proud
to write again; and now that he was home once
more, an impulse had brought him back to her door.
And he had listened to the advice of a woman whom
he had always trusted, and who told him that he
had been wrong and proud, and that he had almost
deserved to lose the woman he loved.

A very pert housemaid with a mob-cap opened
the door; and to Colonel Baxter's enquiry replied
that Miss Marlow was abroad, travelling with friends,
Mr. and Mrs. Bracy and Mr. Jasper Bracy from Bray-
field. She was not expected? O dear no; all letters
were to be sent on to the hotel at Berne. "Here is
the foreign address," says the housemaid, going to a
table and coming back with a piece of paper.

A minute ago it had been on Baxter's lips to ask
her to give him back a letter which he had posted
himself only the day before, addressed to Miss Marlow, at Harpington, not to the Falcon Hotel, at Berne.
But the sight of her writing, of a little flourish to
the F, touched him oddly. When the lively housemaid went on to say that a packet was just a-going,
and Baxter saw his own letter lying on the hall

table, he gave the maid a card and asked her to
put it in as well, and thoughtfully turned on his
heel and walked away. Then he stopped, walked
back a few steps once more along the terrace to a
side window that he remembered, and he stood for
an instant trying to recall a vision of that starry dim
evening when the iron gates were first closed and
he had waited, while Felicia flitted in through that
shuttered window. He still heard her childish sweet
voice; he could remember the pain with which he
left her then; and now—what was there between
them? Nothing. Baxter thought as he walked away
that Felicia had been more really present this time
in remembrance than the last time when he had
really seen her, touched her hand, and found her at
home indeed, but preoccupied, surrounded by adu-
lating sympathisers, dressed in crape, excited, unlike
herself, and passionately sobbing for James's death.
Yes, she had once loved him better than that. It
was not Felicia whom he had really seen that last
time. He *must* see her again, her herself. She would
get his letter; but what good was a letter? It had a
voice perhaps, but no eyes, no ears. The Hôtel
du Faucon at Berne was not a very long way off.
Before he left the terrace, Baxter had made up his
mind to go there.

I wrote this little story down many years ago

now. The people interested me at the time, for
they were all well-meaning folks, moving in a somewhat morbid atmosphere, but doing the best they
could under difficult circumstances. There was the
young couple, who had been engaged from childhood without, as I have said, much knowledge of
anything outside the dreary old home in which Fate
had enclosed their lives. There was an old couple,
whose experience might have taught them better
than to try and twine hymeneal garlands out of dead
men's shoes, strips of parchment, twigs and dried
leaves off their genealogical tree, with a little gold
tinsel for sunshine. The saving clause in it all was
that James Marlow truly loved his cousin Felicia;
but this the old folks scarcely took into account;
and it was for quite different reasons that they de-
creed the two should be one. And then came human
nature in the shape of a very inoffending and unconscious soldier, a widower with one child, a soldier
of fortune without a fortune, as he called himself,
whereas James Marlow, the hero of this little tragedy
(for it *was* a tragedy of some sort), was the heir to
the estate, and a good man, and tenderly attached
to his cousin. But, nevertheless, the little heroine's
heart went away from mousy old Harpington, and
flashed something for itself which neither grandmother nor grandfather had intended, and which Felicia

herself did not quite understand. James Marlow, perhaps, of them all was the person who most clearly realised the facts which concerned these complicated experiences.

Felicia found out her own secret in time, in shame and remorse; and James, who had found it out, kept silence, for he too had a secret, and knew that for him a very short time must break the solemnest engagements. He did full justice to Felicia's impulsive, vivid-hearted nature; to the honesty of the man she preferred to himself.

The three had parted under peculiar circumstances. James had been sent abroad by the doctors as his last chance for life, and before he went he had said something to Felicia, and Baxter not one word. The Captain, as he was then, was faithfully attached to James; he went abroad with his friend, and remained with him while he lived and tended him in those journeys, and administered those delusive prescriptions which were to have cured him. The air was so life-giving, the doctors spoke so confidently, James himself was almost deceived at one time.

His was a wise heart, and a just one, consequently; if he had lived he would have done his part to make those he loved happy, even though their own dream of happiness should not include his own. But he had no chance from the first, ex-

cept, indeed, that of being a good man, and knowing the meaning of a few commonplace words, such
as duty, love, friendship. From a child he was always ailing and sensitive. When he found that his
happiness (it had been christened Felicia some eighteen years before) was gone from him, it made him
languid, indifferent, his pulse ebbed away, not even
African sun could warm him, he would have lived
if he could, but he was not sorry to die; and when
he found he was dying, he sent a message home to
"his sweet happiness," so he spoke of her.

Baxter had come back to England, with his heart
sore for his friend's loss, and neither he nor Felicia,
who had been wearying and pining to see him again,
could find one word, except words of grief. In
those days it had seemed to them both that it would
be wronging James's memory to speak of their own
preoccupations at such a time; so little do people
with the best hearts and intentions trust each other,
or those who have loved them most. Baxter had
not come to Harpington, but to London, where Felicia was staying with her aunt in Queen's Square.
The old butler showed him up the old staircase,
looked round, and then went to the window and
said, "Miss Felicia, you are wanted. Here is Colonel Baxter."

She had come into the room to speak to him,

stepping across the window-sill from the balcony, where she had been sitting. How well he remembered it, and the last time they had been there together. That was in the evening, and Jem had been alive. Now it was morning, and Felicia wore her black dress; a burning autumn morning, striking across the withered parks in broad lines of dusky light. They flooded through the awnings, making the very crape and blackness twinkle. But Felicia's face somehow put out the light; it was pale, and set, and wan. There was no appeal in it now. She frightened Baxter for a moment; then, when he saw her hands tremble, a great longing came to him to hold them fast, to be her help and comforter once more and to befriend this forlorn though much-loved woman. He talked on quickly to hide his emotion. He gave her the few details she wanted.

"Jem told me to come and see you," he concluded. "He thought I might perhaps be your friend, Felicia," said Baxter, "and he sent you his love."

Baxter turned pale, and his voice faltered; he hardly knew how to give the remainder of James's message, which was to tell Felicia that she must let Baxter take care of her now. James sent them both his blessing. Perhaps he might have said the words, but the door opened, and another Miss Marlow

came bustling in; Aunt Mary Anne, a stout, beam-
ing, good-natured, and fussy lady, with many bugles
and ornaments and earrings, and a jet-bespangled
bonnet rather awry, and two fat black kid hands
put out.

"Here he is! Here is our Captain. How is he?
They told me you were here; how glad I am to see
you. You two poor dears have been having a sad
talk, I daresay. Well, it is a good thing got over.
It's no use dwelling on what can't be helped. You
don't look well, Baxter; you must come and let us
nurse you up." And then, as she grasped Colonel
Baxter's hands, "We must make the best of what is
left us. Eh, Felicia?" said the fat lady, who hated
anything in the shape of grief, and only tolerated
its bugles and lighter ornaments. "No, we won't
speak of the past—better not—but tell us how long
you can stay." And the old aunt, who took things
so easy, began to wink and nod at the poor little
passionate-hearted girl, to whom all this seemed
like some horrible mockery—like ribald talk in a
sacred place. Felicia and Baxter both began to
shrink before the old lady's incantations. Felicia
had wiped her tears, and stood silent and dull.
Baxter was cold, vexed, and ajar. He saw Felicia's
averted looks; his own face grew dark. He could
not remain in London; he said he had not yet been

to his own home. His little girl was at Brighton,
with his cousin Emily. And while Miss Marlow the
elder, disappointed in her well-meant efforts to cheer
up the young people, was remonstrating, and scold-
ing, and threatening to appeal to Flora Bracy, whoever she might be, Baxter stood, looking abstractedly
at Felicia, and Felicia drew herself away farther and
farther.

"Perhaps you will let me hear from you, when
you can see me again," said Baxter, taking leave
with some sudden change of manner.

"Yes, yes; you shall hear from us," cried Miss
Marlow the elder, giving him a friendly tap on the
shoulder; young Miss Marlow dropped her eyes,
with a sigh, and did not speak. And so he had
walked away and out into the street, disappointed.
It had not been the meeting he had hoped; it had
not been the meeting Felicia hoped. They had
neither of them made a sign to the other. Baxter
thought of Felicia day after day, Felicia thought of
Baxter. "You sly thing; I know you will write to
him as soon as you get back, though you won't let
me write now," her aunt used to say; and Felicia
would shake her head.

"It seems to me that, for dear James's sake,
you ought to show him some attention," persists the
old lady.

Was it indeed for James's sake only, or for her own, that Felicia wished to see Baxter? This was a question she could never answer. She went back to Harpington, and day after day Felicia put off writing; and Baxter was too proud to go unsummoned. And then a thousand chances and less generous feelings intervened, and time went on, and on, and on; and James might have never lived for all the good his self-sacrifice had brought about to the two people he held most dear.

CHAPTER II.

FELICIA'S RETROSPECTIONS.

In the first part of my story I have described how Felicia lived at Harpington with her grandmother, old Mrs. Marlow, the original match-maker —a strange and somewhat stony-faced old lady, who did not seem always quite in her right mind. Her presence frightened people away. She seemed to have been years before frozen by some sudden catastrophe, and to be utterly indifferent to everything that happened now. She had no love for Felicia. It was almost as if she resented the poor child's very existence. Felicia's betters were gone; her grandfather, her father, her mother, her young aunts and uncles, a whole blooming company had passed away. What business had Felicia to live on, to gather in her one little hand all the possessions which for years past had been amassed for others?

Sorrow for the dead seemed to take the shape of some dull resentment against the living in this bitter woman's mind. All Felicia's grace and loving readiness failed to touch her. Fay did her best

2*

and kept to her duty, as well as she knew how. It was a silent duty, monotonous, ungrateful; it seemed like gathering figs off thorns, or grapes off thistles, to try and brighten up this gloomy woman. Felicia knew there was one person who would gladly, at a sign from her, respond to the faintest call; but, as I have said, some not unnatural scruple withheld her from sending for him. She hoped he would come to her, but *she* would move no finger, say no word, to bring him. She kept the thought of him as she had done all these years, shyly in the secret recesses of her heart. She was so young that the future was still everything—the present mattered little. Young people seem to have some curious trust in their future consciences, as older ones look back with sympathy to their past selves.

After all, it was not very long before Felicia saw Aurelius again; but not in the way she had hoped to see him. She had ridden into L—— on some commission for her grandmother—I think it was a sleeping draught that the old lady fancied. It was a lovely autumn afternoon; old Caspar snuffed the fresh air; young Felicia sprang into her saddle with more life and spirit than she had felt since their trouble had fallen upon them. Old George was there to follow in his battered blue livery. He opened the gates when Felicia had not jumped down

before him. The two jogged along the country lanes
together, old George's blear eyes faithfully fixed on
Caspar's ragged tail. The road was delightful, white
drifting wreaths of briony seemed to lie like foam
upon the branches, ivies crept green along the
ditches, where the very weeds were turning into
gold and silver, while the branches of the trees overhead were also aglow in the autumnal lights. It
was a sweet triumphant way. The girl's spirit rose
as she cantered along between the garlands that
spread on either side of it. There is one place
where the road from Harpington crosses the road to
L——, just where an old mill stands by a stream
with its garden and farm buildings. The fence was
low, and as Felicia peeped over she could see a
garden full of sweet clustering things mingling with
vegetables, white feathery bushes, and bowers of
purple clematis, and here and there crimson fiery
tongues, darting from their stems along the box-
lined paths and yellow roses against the walls. The
place was well cared for, and seemed full of life
and rest too. She could hear a sound of horses,
and of voices calling and dogs barking in the mill-
yard beyond the garden. The flowers seemed all
the sweeter for the busy people at work. Felicia
began to build up one of her old fancy-pieces as she
lingered for a moment by the hedge; perhaps some

day they might walk there together, and he would look
down into her face and say the time has come, the time
has come.   Then she started, blushed up, tightened
old Caspar's rein again, and set off once more rid-
ing quickly past the old sign-post that pointed to
Harpington with one weather-beaten finger, and to
L——, whither she was going.   There was a third
road leading to the downs—it was only a continua-
tion of the Harpington lane.

The mill was near an hour's ride from L——,
that pretty old country town, with its bustle of new
things cheerfully mixing up with the old—its many
children at play and its many busy people stirring
among the old gables and archways, and its flocks
making confusion in the market.

Felicia left old Caspar to be cared for at the
inn, while she went off upon her shopping, being,
girl-like, delighted with the life and bustle of the
place.   She herself was perhaps not the least pleasant sight there, as she darted in and out of the
old doorways and corners, holding up her long skirt,
and looking out beneath the broad brim of her dark
beaver hat.   It was late before she had done.   The
town clocks were striking six as they turned their
horses' heads towards Harpington.   There is a long
level stretch of road at the foot of the hill, with
poplars growing on either side, and tranquil horizons

between the poplar stems. Felicia trotted on ahead; old George jogged after her, pondering upon his crops and the price of wheat, which he had been discussing in the bar of the Red Lion.

Evening was falling: the oxen looked purple in the light, as they stood staring across the fences at the road and the horses, and slowly tossing their white horns. The shadows under the trees were turning blue, the evening birds were flying across the sky—a tranquil dappled sky, with clouds passing in fleecy banks, while the west spread its crimson wings. All the people were crossing and recrossing the paths to the villages beyond the fields; in one place Felicia could see the boats gliding along the narrow river. Then they came to the old mill at the cross-roads. The garden was resplendent with clear evening light: the great cabbages seemed dilating and showing every vein; each tendril of the vines, wreathed along the wooden palings, stood out vivid and defined. As Felicia advanced, urging old Caspar along, she saw a figure also on horseback coming along the road from Harpington. It was but for a moment, but in that moment Felicia seemed to recognise the rider: his square shoulders, the slouch of his broad hat. He crossed the highway, and took the lane leading to the downs: he did not look to the right or to the left. Felicia's

heart gave a throb. She suddenly slashed old
Caspar into a canter, and reached the corner where
she thought she had just seen Baxter pass. She
looked up and down. "Did not somebody go by,
George?" Felicia said, turning round to the old gardener. "I can see no one in the lane. It must a'
been a goast," said old George, staring, "or maybe
it wer' a man that leapt the fence onto yon field:
there'll be a short cut along by that thar way," says
George, who had followed his master, the late Squire,
along many a short cut and long road. Felicia said
no more; she turned Caspar's head towards home,
and the old horse stepped out, knowing his way
back. To Felicia the way seemed suddenly very
long. The road was dusty and bare; the garlands
seemed to have lost their fragrant bloom. Her
grandmother was up when she got back. Tea was
laid in the parlour, and the windows were open on
to the terrace.

"There has been someone to see us," said Mrs.
Marlow. "That Baxter was here. He is going
away again to India. Have you got me my sleeping draught."

"Did he leave *no* message for me; nothing?"
said Felicia.

"He left his card," said the old lady. "Take
care, don't shake the bottle; what are you about! I

want a good night's rest. That man talked about James, he upset me. I had to send him away. He would have kept me awake at night if I had let him talk on any longer." And then Mrs. Marlow hobbled off to her old four-post bed, crumpling up Baxter's card in her fingers. "I *must* see you once more," he had written upon it; "send me one line." Mrs. Marlow threw the card into her fire-place. Felicia never saw the pencil words. She was left alone—quite alone she said to herself bitterly. He had left her no word, he was gone without a thought of her, and everything seemed forlorn once more.

Old Mrs. Marlow survived her grandson for a year; half imbecile, never quite relenting to the poor little granddaughter, and then she too passed away, and Felicia inherited the old house and the broad stubble-fields and the farm-yards and hay-cocks, among which she and her cousin James had both grown up together. And now Felicia belonged to that sad company of heiresses, with friends and a banker's account, and consideration and liberty, in place of home and loving interest and life multiplied by others.

She came; she went; she travelled abroad. She was abroad when Baxter came to Harpington for the second time in vain. He had been in India hard at work, and little Felicia had been leading her own

life for the last three years. Everything seemed to
be hers except the things which might have made
everything dear to her. She had scarcely been conscious of any want; she was never alone—never
neglected. Events came by every post, twopenny
pleasures, sixpenny friendships, small favours asked
and cheap thanks returned. All this had not improved her, and yet she was the same Felicia after
all that Baxter remembered so fondly, as he walked
away from the door.

CHAPTER III.

ON THE TERRACE AT BERNE.

THERE is a stone basin full of water in an old city in Switzerland, over which a shady stream of foliage waves against the sun. The city arms are emblazoned upon the stone, and the flood of green overflows its margin. In the autumn the leaves glow, gleam, change into flame or ashes, tendrils hang illumined over the brimming fountain, which reflects the saffron and the crimson overhead. The towns-women come and fill their brazen pans and walk away leisurely, swinging their load and splashing the footway. The sloping street leads to a cathedral, of which the bells come at stated hours, suddenly breaking the habitual silence, and echoing from gable to gable.

A young English lady passing by one autumn day went and stood for an instant by the fountain, leaning over its side. The naïads, in their Sunday boddices and well-starched linen, who were already there filling their brazen cans, watched her with some interest, and looked curiously at the stranger's bright startled eyes, her soft grey felts and feathers, and her quick all-pervading looks. They themselves were of the placid broad-faced, broad-shouldered race of naïads who people Switzerland, who haunt the fountains; who emerge from châlets and caves with sparkling cups in their hands; who invite you to admire their fresh water-courses through kaleido-scopes of various tints.

There is a certain sameness, but an undeniable charm about Swiss maidens, especially on Sundays, when they put on their pretty silver ornaments, plait their shining tails of hair, while their fresh and blooming faces certainly do credit to their waters. Felicia had been standing interested and absorbed for some minutes. She was watching the stream flow on; wondering whether life hard won in the Bernese valleys would not be more satisfying on the whole than it seemed to her day by day, flowing, unheeded, in her own lonely and luxurious home. Presently she caught a whispered comment from one nymph to another, "She is not alone; here is the company coming from the Falcon to find her." Then Miss Marlow started, looked up, hastily turned away, and began walking determinedly away along the street. She had come out to avoid her company, that was the truth. For a week she had been travelling with them and glad to be in their society, but that morning a letter had reached her from home which had strung her to some other key, and which made her want to be alone for a little to realise her own mind, to hear her own voice, and to listen to that of an old friend speaking across five years. Was Baxter right when he thought that a letter was nothing? his letter certainly had a voice for Felicia. They had never had one word of explanation before or since they parted. There had been no promise given on either side; and yet she had considered herself in some implied way bound to this absent person whom she had not seen twenty times before James Marlow died, and who had not come back to her, except once with a shy, cruel, stiff message.

Felicia flitted away, as preoccupied as Baxter himself had been with certain events of former years. The houses on either side of the street stood upon their arches, the broad roofs cast their shadows, the quaint turrets turned to daily domestic use protruded from the corners, pigeons flew whirring across her footsteps. The street was called the *Street of the Preachers*. Felicia spelt it out, written high against a gable, and as she read the words all the cathedral chimes began preaching overhead, sounding, vibrating, swinging through the air; the sunlight broke out more brightly, doors opened and figures passed out on their way to the Cathedral, from whence a little procession came slowly to meet her. It was headed by a sleeping baby lying peacefully frilled and pinned on to a huge lace pillow, with a wreath of silver flowers round its little head. On its placid little breast a paper was laid with a newly bestowed name carefully written out, with many simple-minded flourishes. . . .

A little farther on a closed house opened, and a tall and solemn-looking personage issued forth, some quaint ghost of a past century, with a short Geneva gown, and a huge starched ruffle round his chin, walking with a deliberate step. The apparition crossed the piazza, passed under the statue (it seemed to be brandishing a bronze sword in its country's defence, against the scattered and mutilated wreaths that lay on the steps at the horse's feet); then the cathedral doors opened wide to receive this quaint ghost of another time and faith. It passed on with one or two people who had been standing round about. The bells gave a last leap of welcome, and then were silent, and the doors closed with a solemn bang. . . . Felicia noted it all, interested in spite of herself, and her own abstractions. Sometimes in our perplexities the lives of other people seem to come to reassure us. Have they not too been anxious, happy, died, lived, walked from house to house, stood outside and inside cathedral porches, as little Felicia stood now, staring at the saints over the doorway? It was a whole generation of ornamental sanctities, all in beatitude no doubt, and independent of circumstances: some were placidly holding their heads in their hands, some contemplating their racks, others kneeling on perilous ledges. Felicia was no saintly character, but she had gone through a certain gentle martyrdom in her life, short as it was. Now she took a letter out of her pocket, and looked at it thoughtfully, and read it once again. It had been sent on to her from her own house, and had been waiting for her at the hotel when she arrived that morning, with a pile of bills, invitations, demisemiquavers of notes, in the midst of all of which this chord suddenly sounded:—

"My dear Miss Marlow—I have thought it possible that you have understood the reason which has prevented me from troubling you all this long time, and which made me wish for some sign from you, before I again asked to see you. Before I left England it seemed to me more and more difficult to see you or to come unasked to Harpington without probable misconstruction. In India one report reached me after another; and some not unnatural feeling prevented a proud man from wishing to appear to put himself into competition with a crowd of others, whose personal advantages seemed undeniable—and I remained sorry and disappointed, and knowing that it was my own fault that I had not seen you once more. I now think that for many reasons, my own peace of mind being one of them, this indefinite estrangement between two old friends should not continue. I am at home again for six months, and staying at The Cottage with Lucy and my cousin Emily Flower. I shall come to-morrow to see you, and to hear from your own lips upon what terms you would wish henceforward that we should meet.

"Believe me always

"The Cottage,   Faithfully yours,
  "Harpington.   A. H. BAXTER."

It was a difficult letter to read; was it very difficult to answer? Felicia was both hurt and touched; hurt by the long mistrust and doubt which was implied by this delay, touched by this long-delayed confidence. If the writer had only come to her as James had no doubt intended him to do, helped her in her hours of loneliness and sorrow, proved himself the stay and comfort for which she had longed, how happy they might have been all this time; if instead of speculating anxiously, com-

paring his advantages with those of others who were
nothing to her, he had but forgotten himself for her,
how different these last few years would have seemed
to her, how much less sad, less drearily gay, less
noisy, less confused. She had had a right to be
hurt, to give no sign.—Did he deserve forgiveness
now?—If he had really loved her would he have
treated her so cruelly? or did he only think that she
loved him. Her eyes filled with tears, tender angry
drops that she impatiently dashed away.

Felicia walked on beyond the cathedral gates to
the terrace close by; a delightful autumn garden for
children and old people, with a wide valley and a
line of distant hills beyond the walls. All the leaves
were falling from the trees, and the brown chestnuts
were dropping with the sudden swift gusts of wind;
the country flushed with a bright tumult of sunshine
and clouds: the river rolled with a full silver rush;
the streets below were piled up against the very foot
of the dizzy terrace walls; as seen from the high
cliff the Bernese men and women seemed like toys
for children to play with, tiny figures that passed
and repassed, intent upon their liliput affairs, upon
rolling a barrel or turning a wheel, or upon piling
a stack of wood; in windows and garrets, upon terraces and outstanding balconies, everywhere people
were occupied, passing and repassing. The whole

business of their microscopic life seemed scarcely so important as the children's game on the cathedral terrace—they were shouting as they ran, and picking up dry leaves and brown shining chestnuts that fell from the trees.

Felicia was standing against the terrace wall, still reading her letter, still thinking over the meaning of its somewhat abrupt sentences. They were not unlike Baxter's own way of speaking, stiff, abrupt, melting now and then for an instant, and then repelling again. The girl covered her eyes with her hand, trying to recall the vivid past more vividly. She was changed, this she knew, since those childish days when her whole heart's emotion had overpowered her so easily, and she had appealed in vain against her cruel condemning fate; she wanted something more now than she had wanted then; she had learned to mistrust her own impulses as well as those of the people she lived with. She wanted to trust, as well as to feel; she wanted proof as well as the expression of good-will. Poor little Felicia, it was not for nothing that she had been an heiress all this while, warned, flattered, surrounded, educated by cruel experience. All that was past now in her short life seemed suddenly in existence again, came as a wave in between her and the man she had loved; it seemed to float them asunder as

she conjured up his image; and so it happened, by
some curious chance, that they met. As she wiped
her eyes, her heart seemed to cease beating for an
instant. What extraordinary realisation was this?—
who was this coming across the shadow of the
chestnut tree? Felicia, looking up with a start,
found herself face to face with a tall man who had
slowly followed her all this time; the hand that had
written the letter was held out to her, and the letter
seemed to take voice and life, and to say, "It is I;
don't look frightened." The strangest things cease to be
strange after a moment. Miss Marlow was accustomed
to face possibilities, and as for Colonel Baxter, had
he not followed her all the way from the fountain?

"It is really you!" she said, looking more lovely
than he had ever seen her look before.

Colonel Baxter smiled admiringly, and held out
his hand. Miss Marlow flushed crimson, and looked
up into his face an instant before she took it. He
was altogether unaltered; he did not look older, he
did not look gladder. He was moved, but less so
than she was; his dark face seemed pale somehow,
and thin; she could not see very clearly, she was
too much troubled and excited.

First meetings are curious things, all the long
habit of separation seems still to be there; all the
long days that have come to divide, the very anxie-

3*

ties and preoccupations that have made the time so heavy, now seem to thrust themselves in between those who have yearned for each other's presence, and the absent are come home at last, but as people are not all gone when they first depart, so they are not always quite come when they meet after long separation.

"I have just been reading your letter, Colonel Baxter," said Felicia quietly, and regaining her composure.

"I heard you were abroad from your housekeeper," said Colonel Baxter, "and I thought that— that I might as well follow my letter," he said, with an odd expression. All this time he had been so afraid of what Felicia might think; and now she was there before him, more charming, more beautiful even than he had remembered her. His scruples were all forgotten; they seemed unkind, almost cruel. Her eyes fell beneath his look, her face changed, a dazzle of sunlight came before his eyes, it may have been the falling leaves, the wind stirring among the branches, it may have been his own long pent emotion, but it seemed to him suddenly as if he could read what was passing in her mind, as if some vibration had swept away all outward conventional signs. He was a silent man usually, not given to much expression, but at this moment the feeling that had long been in his heart overmastered everything else. What was her money to him at that instant, or his own disadvantages? He even tried to remember them, but he could not recall one single impediment between them.

"You do not know what a struggle it has been to me to keep away! Can you forgive me?" he said; going straight to the point—ignoring all he had meant to say—to explain—to withhold.

"I do not quite forgive you," said Felicia, smiling with tears, and once more responding to this new never-forgotten affection, by some instinct against which she could not struggle. As they stood there a swift western gale began to blow, the leaves showered from the trees, the chestnuts dropped over the terrace and beyond the wall, the children scampered through the changing lights. What had not happened in this moment's meeting. "No, I can't quite forgive you," repeated Miss Marlow. "Where have you been all this time? What have you been doing? What were you thinking of?"

He could scarcely answer for a minute, though he looked so calm. He was more really overcome perhaps than she was; he was blaming himself unsparingly, wondering at his pride, the infatuation which had kept them apart, wondering at her outcoming pardoning sweetness and welcome. Baxter, who had been embittered by various mischances; Felicia Marlow, whose pretty little head had been somewhat turned of late by the dazzling compliments and adulations which she had met with, had both forgotten everything in the present, and met each other with their best and truest selves; surprised by the chance which seemed at last to have favoured them. Details did not exist for either of them. At that minute Felicia felt that the future was there facing her with the serious and tender looks. Baxter also thought that at last, leaving all others, she had come straight to him, confiding with perfect trust. With a silent triumph, almost painful in its intensity, he held her hand close in his.

"Nothing shall ever come between us again," he said. "Nothing—no one." Was Fate displeased by his presumption? As he spoke a cheerful chorus reached them from behind, a barking of dogs, a chatter of voices. Felicia blushing, drew her hand away from Baxter. A scraping of feet, and in one instant the couple seem surrounded—ladies, gentlemen, parasols, a pugdog. "Here you are, we saw you from the place; why did you run away?" cries a voice. Felicia, with gentle confusion, began to name everybody: "Mrs. Bracy, Mr. Jasper, Mr. Bracy, Miss Harrow. Dear Mrs. Bracy, you remember our James's friend, Colonel Baxter."

"We have met in Queen's Square," said Mrs. Bracy, with her most graciously concealed vexation. Had she not brought Felicia abroad expressly to avoid Colonels of any sort?

CHAPTER IV.

BEARS IN THEIR DENS.

Baxter found it almost impossible to adjust himself suddenly to these unexpected circumstances, to these utter strangers, complacently dispersing his very heart's desire—so it seemed to him.

The results seemed so very small, compared to the intolerable annoyance inflicted upon himself. His was not the best nor the most patient of tempers, and he would gladly have dropped Mr. and Mrs. Bracy, Mr. Jasper, and Miss Harrow too over the terrace at a sign from Felicia. But she gave no sign, she seemed, could it be, almost relieved by their coming. In one instant all his brief dream, his shelter of hope seemed shaken, dispersed: not one of these people but came in between him and her; they did it on purpose. Couldn't they see that they were in the way? I am not sure that Mrs. Bracy did not do it on purpose. She took the Colonel in at a comprehensive glance. Cold, clear, that look seemed to him to be a wall of well-polished plate-glass, let down between him and Felicia, who

had in some confusion accepted Mr. Bracy's arm,
and was already walking away and leaving Baxter
to his fate. "We are going to the Bears," cried
Mr. Bracy, over his shoulder. "Flora, are you equal
to the walk, my love? Jasper, take care of your
aunt. What are you looking at?"

Jasper started at this address. He had been
standing motionless, gazing up at the sky, and he
now turned round. He was a young man about five
or six and twenty, peculiar in appearance, and curiously dressed; his hair was frizzed out something in
the same fashion as his aunt's own locks. He wore
an orange cravat, a blue linen shirt, rings upon his
fore-fingers, buckles to his shoes, a silver pin was
fastened to his wide felt hat. He was handsome,
with one of those silly expressions which come from
too much intelligent detail.

"I beg pardon," said he. "That amber cloud
floating in ultra-marine called me irresistibly;" and
he pointed and stood quite still for an instant, as
actors do at the play, who have, of course, to em-
phasise their movements as well as their words.
Felicia had no great sense of humour, and to her
Jasper Bracy's performance was most serious and
important. Baxter could hardly help laughing, at
least he might have laughed if he had been less
disturbed.

Mrs. Bracy was a lady of about fifty, she must have been handsome once. Her dark hair was nearly black, her features still retained a somewhat regal dignity of hook and arch, her brow was shiny and of the same classic proportions as her conversation.

"Do you wish to see the bears? Do you not agree with me, Colonel Baxter, that it is a cruelty to keep such noble animals in durance vile?" said Flora, turning to Aurelius, who looked very black and brown, and likely to growl himself.

"What do you say to a study from the life, my dear aunt?" said Jasper, joining in. Some friends of mine are going to Poland bear-shooting, next month. I should be glad to join them and to make a few sketches from the dead carcase."

"Jasper, do not talk of such horrible necessities," said his aunt. "My husband must show you some lines I wrote upon 'Living Force restrained by the Inert,'" continued she, with a roll of her glossy eyes, "which bear upon the stern necessities of Fate. Colonel Baxter, you do not seem to catch my meaning."

Felicia, who was a few steps ahead, turned at this moment, hearing Mrs. Bracy's remonstrances; and the kind grey eyes beamed some little friendly signal to the poor disconcerted Colonel, who tried to overmaster his ill-humour, and to attend to the authoress's quotations, and abruptly asked what was meant by "the inert."

"Bars, bars," said Flora, "those bars of circumstances that weigh upon us all; upon you, I dare say—upon myself. What is *this* but a bar, through which no woman can pass?" and she held up her fat finger, with the wedding-ring which Mr. Bracy had doubtless placed there.

While Mrs. Bracy, now well launched in metaphor, reveled on from sentence to sentence, Baxter's attention wandered; he was watching the slight graceful figure ahead flitting over the stones by Mr. Bracy's dumpy little form, only he listened when Felicia's friend began to speak of Felicia. They had left the terrace by this time, and were walking down a shady side street. "Dear child," Mrs. Bracy was saying, and she pointed to Felicia with her parasol, "those who have her welfare at heart must often wonder what fate has in store for one so strangely gifted. You may think what an anxious charge it is for *me*, who am aware of all Felicia's exquisite refinement and sensitiveness of disposition. I have known her from childhood, although circumstances at one time divided us" (the circumstances being that until three years before Mrs. Bracy had never taken the slightest

notice of little Felicia). "There are many persons
who, from a subtle admixture of feelings, are attracted
by our sweet heiress," continued the lady. "I will
not call them interested, and yet in my heart I
cannot but doubt their motives. You, Colonel Baxter, will, I am sure, agree with me in despising the
mercenary advances of these—shall I call them?—
soldiers of fortune." Aurelius could hardly force
himself to listen to the end of Mrs. Bracy's tirade,
and gave her one black angry look, then suddenly
strode on two or three steps, joined Felicia, and
resolutely kept by her side. She looked up, hearing
his step, but though she smiled she continued silent.
She would not, indeed, she could not, talk to Baxter
about indifferent subjects. Just at that moment she
wanted to breathe, to collect her nerves and her
mind. One vivid impression after another seemed
to overcome her, Aurelius attracted and frightened
her too; he seemed to have seized upon her, and
half-willingly, half-reluctantly, she had let herself be
carried away. It was a new Aurelius, a new Felicia,
since that moment upon the terrace. Mr. Bracy
rattled on with his usual good-humoured inconse-
sequence. Mrs. Bracy caught them up at every
opportunity. Jasper, who prided himself upon his
good breeding, showed no sign of the annoyance he
may perhaps have felt at the unexpected advent of

this formidable arrival, for it was to charm Felicia
that these strange attitudes and ornaments were
assumed, and that Jasper sang his song. By degrees
Felicia's composure returned. She was able to talk
and be interested as the others were, to look at the
dresses of the peasant people, at the little children
in their go-carts, at the streams above the bridge
and below it, at the green river rushing between
the terraces and the balconies; she was able to
throw buns to the bears, and to laugh when they
rolled over on their brown woolly backs, with crimson jaws wide stretched; she was still a child in
some things, and when she caught sight of the
Colonel's face she almost resented his vexed look.
Why didn't he laugh at the bears' antics. Poor
fellow; Mrs. Bracy's conversation might well account
for any depression on his part. She seemed to
scintillate with allusions.

Fortune hunters? Felicia's rare delicacies of
feeling, and her own deep sympathies, which enabled her and her only to know what would be
suited to that young creature's requirements; she
seemed to have taken such complete stock of the
poor little thing, that Aurelius wondered what would
be left for any other human being. He knew it was
absurd to be so sensitive. He might have trusted
the woman who had loved him for years and years,

but at this moment Mrs. Bracy's monotonous voice was ringing in his brain.

It seemed to him, notwithstanding all his experience and long habit of life and trust in Felicia, that he had been a fool. Was he to subject himself to this suspicion for any woman's sake? Had he placed his hopes upon some one utterly and entirely beyond his reach? Was not that the refrain of it all? Did Felicia mean him to bear alone? She did not seem to interfere; she avoided him; and yet, surely, they had understood each other when they had met only a few minutes ago. He could endure it no longer. He came up to Miss Marlow, and said abruptly: "I am going back to the hotel now; will you come with me?"

"We are all coming," said Felicia, looking eagerly around; "don't leave us."

"I cannot stand your friend's conversation any longer," said Aurelius, not caring who heard him. "She is the most intolerable woman."

Felicia seemed to be gazing attentively at the bears, as she bent far over the railing. "You should not speak like that," she said, very much annoyed. "They are all so kind to me. What do you want?"

"I want to see you," he said, standing beside her. "I want to talk to you; and I wonder you don't see how cruelly you are behaving, keeping me in this horrible suspense."

"One more sugarplum, my Felicia, to give your four-footed friends," here says a voice just behind them, and a fat hand is thrust between them with a peppermint between the finger and thumb.

Baxter turned angrily away. "This is unbearable," he muttered.

Felicia looked after him reproachfully; he walked straight off; he crossed the place, he never looked back; he left her, feeding the bears with sugarplums; left her to Mrs. Bracy, pointing out the advantages of national liberty, and the tints of the mountains, to Felicia, to Miss Harrow, to anyone who would listen. Jasper, his aunt knew by experience, was not a good listener; he would compose himself into an attitude of profound attention, but his eye always wandered before long.

I suppose Felicia wanted a little time to think it all over, and to understand what had happened, and that was why she took no decisive step concerning her new lover. A curious feeling—surprise and confidence and quiet expectancy—seemed to have come over her. Baxter's impatient words had startled her. It was something she was unprepared for. Was this love, this sudden unaccustomed rule? —was she in future to be at another person's call?

She had not taken the Colonel's character into account; she had never thought about his character, to tell the truth, only that he had come, that the story of her youth had begun again. He had come as she knew he would, and she had all but promised to be his wife. She did not want to go back from her word; but she wanted to wait a little bit, to put off facing this terrible definite fact a little longer, now that it had come so near. She had got into a habit of waiting. He ought to be happy: what more could he want her to say? And she wanted to be happy also, to rest and enjoy her happiness, and not to be carried breathless away by his impatient strength of will.

CHAPTER V.

THE FALCON HOTEL.

THE Falcon, at Berne, is a quiet old-fashioned place, very silent and restful, and reached by flights of white stone steps. There are echoes, panels, galleries, round an old court, and a kitchen which is raised high above the ground. You can see the cook's white caps through a gable window, and taste the cook's good cheer in a paneled dining-room, at the end of a long empty table.

Now and then you hear a piano's distant flourishes, and if you go to the windows you see a sleepy old piazza, and the serious people sauntering by, and your bedroom windows across the street.

Aurelius, who was moodily passing the deserted dining-room, was seized upon by Mr. Bracy, who had come in to order some refreshments. "Do you dine with us at the *table-d'hôte?*" said the little gentleman, "there is no one else. My wife finds that absolute quiet is necessary to her. The afflatus is easily startled—easily startled away. I have known Flora lose some of her finest ideas through the in-

opportune entrance of a waiter or the creaking of a
door. I myself one night thoughtlessly attempted to
whistle that chorus out of Faust—(after all who is
there like Gounod in these days?)—but the result
was distressing in the extreme. I shall never forget
watching the subsequent wandering about the room
in a vain attempt to recall the interrupted thoughts."

"Do you live in this part of the house?" interrupted Aurelius.

"Come and see our rooms, we are opposite: the
ladies are gone up to the top of the house to watch
the sunset," said the friendly little man. "Charming girl, your friend Miss Marlow; so is Georgina
Harrow, a person of rare amiability of disposition.
Ah! here is the waiter. At *quel heur table-d'hôte*
to-day?"

Aurelius left Mr. Bracy absorbed in the various
merits of private and public refections, and crossed
the street, and went in at the arched door opposite,
and walked up the stone flights of the opposite
house, now darkening with all the shadows of evening. He climbed straight up with steady footsteps
to the upper storey; and there through an open door
he saw, as he had hoped, some heads crowding together, and looking through an open window at a
faint azure sky and all its dying day-lights; Mrs.
Bracy was busily pointing out each tint in turn.

Jasper was criticising the colours, and comparing them with various bits of blue and red rag which he produced from his pockets. Miss Harrow was listening in admiration.

One person had heard Baxter's footsteps, and Felicia, guessing by some instinct that it was Aurelius, slipped unnoticed out of her corner and turned quietly to meet him, with all the evening's soft radiance shining in her eyes. Her sweet truthful look of welcome touched him and reassured him not a little; he forgot his irritation; for the moment he did not speak, neither did she, he could not waste this happy minute in reproach, and indeed he knew as she did that the whole company would surround them at the first spoken word. As they stood side by side, silent, leaning against the wall, the shadows came deeper, the little room was full of peace, and a sort of tranquillising evening benediction seemed to fall upon their hearts; he could hear her quick gentle breath, though her head was turned away. It was no idle fancy, no vague hope taking shape in her imagination. Felicia was there, and she did not repulse him, and met him with a welcome of her own.

"Why, Colonel Baxter, have you been here all this time?" cries Mrs. Bracy, suddenly wheeling round and facing the two as they stood in the dusky corner.

4*

Felicia came to dinner that day looking prettier than ever, and happier than they had seen her yet, although the young heiress was on the whole a cheerful traveller. At home she might be silent and oppressed; but abroad the change, the different daily colours and words, the new and altered ways and things, all amused her and distracted the somewhat hypochondriacal phantoms which had haunted her lonely house—home it could scarcely be called. Baxter might have been happy too had he so chosen, if he had accepted the good things as they came to him with patience and moderation, and not wished to hurry and to frighten his happiness away. But although that five minutes' unexpressed understanding in the garret had soothed his impatient soul, the constant society of Mr. and Mrs. Bracy, the artistic powers of Mr. Jasper, the cultivated observation of Miss Harrow, all seemed to exasperate his not very easy temper. He was very much in earnest, he felt that his whole happiness was at stake. And to be treated to a few sugarplums when he was asking for daily bread, was not a system calculated to soothe a man of Aurelius' temper. Felicia was kind, gay in her most childish mood that evening. Jasper, who seemed to be on the most excellent terms with her, kept up an artistic conversation about the poignant painters of the present age, as opposed to the subtle

school of philosophic submission, while Mrs. Bracy
on the other side asked the colonel many questions
about the Vedas, and the dreamy Orient, and the
moral cultivation of the Zenanas.

The only other people at the table were some
Germans, one of whom was recounting to the others
a colossal walk he contemplated across his plate of
cutlets and brown potatoes. The little Scheidegg,
the waterfall of Lauterbrunnen, the dizzy height of
Mürren to be reached that same evening. "It is a
colossal expedition," says the athlete, with a glance
at the company. "Pfui, Pfui!" cry the others, with
a sort of admiring whistle.

Mrs. Bracy was preparing to take a parting leave
of the colonel that evening; but as Felicia said good-
night Baxter held her hand and said quite simply
before them all, "Is this good-bye, Felicia; may I
not come to Interlaken with you?"

"Why not," said Felicia, demurely, "if you have
time to spare; we are going by the early train. They
say the lake of Thun is lovely."

"I am sure Colonel Baxter will prove a delightful and most unexpected addition to our party,"
cried Mrs. Bracy, not without asperity. "Interlaken
is a charming place; it is more suited for invalids
like myself, who cannot attempt real mountain ex-
peditions than for *preux chevaliers*, but if your friend

will be content, dearest Felicia, to potter with my
old husband—forgive me, Egbert—we will escort
him to the various pavilions round about the hotel."

"I have no doubt I shall be well looked after,"
said Colonel Baxter, with a somewhat ambiguous
gratitude, as he bowed good-night, and walked off
with a candle. Felicia's consent had made his heart
leap with silent gladness; he no longer minded
Mrs. Bracy's jibes. His bedroom was in the same
house as the Bracys' apartments. It was on the
ground floor, and the windows opened on a rustling
and beshadowed garden, where lilac trees waved
upon the starry sky, and striving poplars started
ghostlike and dim; close shrouds of ivy veiled the
walls. Felicia's window was lighted up; and as
Baxter paced the walks smoking his cigar, and
watching the smoke mounting straight into the air,
he caught her voice from time to time, and the
mellifluous accompaniment of Mrs. Bracy's contralto
notes: he could not hear their conversation, but a
word or two reached him now and then, as he
walked along. Presently something made him wince,
alone though he was, dark and solitary as the garden might be; he ceased to puff at the cigar, for an
instant he listened. "My money, my money," Felicia
was repeating; "I know that people think I am
rich;" and then the steps Felicia also had been

listening to, and which somehow she had identified with Baxter, the steps went away and came no more; and the garden was left quite solitary and dark, with its thick shrubs and silent lilac trees, and strange night-dreams.

"Good-night, dear Mrs. Bracy," says the girl, starting from her seat. "How shall I thank you for all your kindness to me. Don't be anxious; I am *sure* no one here ever thinks about my fortune, or about anything but being good to me." But alas! Baxter was not there to hear her.

———

CHAPTER VI.

EN VOYAGE.

PRINGLE, Felicia's maid, did not call her mistress next morning till a very short time before the omnibus was starting for the station; and Felicia, who had lain awake half the night, jumped up half asleep, and proceeded to dress as quickly as she could. They were only just in time. Mr. Bracy was impatiently stamping on the pavement in an agony of punctuality. Jasper had walked on, they said. His luggage was there — three large bags, red, blue, and yellow, with which he habitually travelled. The intelligent Georgina, calm, brown, composed, was sitting in her corner, looking perfectly unmoved. Mrs. Bracy was also installed, checking over the various umbrellas and parcels. She was evidently ruffled: with poetic natures crossness verges on tragedy, and becomes very alarming at times.

"I'm so sorry," said Felicia; and she looked vaguely round, and to her surprise, and disappoint-

ment too, discovered no sign of Colonel Baxter.
"Where is Colonel Baxter?" she said.

"My dear, how can I tell you?" said Mrs. Bracy,
who was in devout hopes that he had been left behind; and Flora stared at Felicia as if in some surprise at her question.

Felicia flushed up; this was not what she had
intended. "Mrs. Bracy, we must go back," said
the young lady very much agitated. "I promised
that he should come with us. What will he think?"

"What is there to prevent Colonel Baxter from
coming with us, if he chooses," said the elder lady
with freezing politeness. "Certainly, if you wish it,
I will desire the omnibus to return."

Felicia was just preparing to say that at all
events Pringle should remain with a message, when
the object of all this discussion stood up at a street
corner to let them pass.

His luggage was also piled on the top of the
omnibus, with Jasper's rainbow bags, and he had
walked the short distance from the hotel to the
railway station.

Felicia, seeing him, was satisfied at once; her
sudden energy of opposition passed away; and when
they all met at the station she greeted him smiling
and composed, gave him her hand and her hand-
bag with its many silver flagons.

Baxter could not find a place in the same carriage with Felicia; he climbed up upon the roof,
where he sat smoking his cigar, and thinking over a
short journey they had once taken together, six
years before. Then it was Fate that had separated
them, honour, every feeling of affection and gratitude; now, only her will and the interference of a
foolish woman kept them apart. From where he
sat he looked down upon Jasper, who stood outside
the carriage door upon a sort of platform with a
rail; the artist was hatless, he wished his hair to
stream upon the wind.

"Take care, Jasper. Come in here," cries Mrs.
Bracy, who had just sent off the Colonel, and declared she must have space for her two fat feet
upon the opposite seat, and that there was no room
for anyone else in the carriage.

But Jasper said he preferred the rhythm of
motion as it thrilled him where he stood.

A pretty little railway runs between the smiling
valleys that lead from Berne to Interlaken.

Felicia looked out of the window well pleased
by the pleasant sights and aspect of the road.

The railway meets a steamer waiting by a certain smiling green landing-place; and all the passengers issue from the train and go on board, and
look over the sides of the boat into deep sweet

waters lapping the shore, and calmly flowing in long silver ripples across the lake. On either side the green banks are full and overflowing. White pensions stand in gardens; people come down to the steps to see the steamer pass. Everything tells of peace, of a placid, prosperous comfort.

Baxter found Felicia a place by an American lady who was pointing out the various scenes of interest with an alpenstock, and the help of a Baedeker, to two young ladies her charges.

"Oh, Miss Cott, is this the page?" enquire her pupils. "What is the exact distance per rail from Berne to the steamer?"

"Page 47," says Miss Cott, rapidly turning over the leaves.

The steamer started off; all the people clustering on board flapped their wings, and hummed their song in the sunshine as it streamed above the awning. The Swiss ladies accepted a respectful share of their husbands' conversation; the American ladies, on the contrary, took the lead. There was one stout and helpless personage, covered with rings and many plaits of false hair, to whom Felicia had taken a great dislike, until a little brown-faced girl with earrings ran up and began to kiss the ugly cheeks and to smoothe the woman's tumbled locks.

"Look at that child," said Felicia; "how fond she seems to be of the horrid old woman! I am sure I never could tolerate such a mother."

"And yet you care for *her*," said Baxter, looking with no friendly glances at Mrs. Bracy advancing to join them. "Oh, Felicia! won't you tell her that you are going to belong to me, not to her? You must choose between us, you see," he said with a smile.

"How can you speak so absurdly?" she said, turning away hurt; "how mistrustful, how unkind you are!"

She did not make allowances for his diffidence, for his boundless admiration, for his natural wish for certainty now that the die was cast. The Colonel, who had less life before him than Felicia, more experience of its chances and disappointments, more intensity of feeling to urge him on, might well be more impatient. He had kept her waiting; did the malicious little creature mean him to feel her power now and to take her wilful vengeance? Her cousin James had spoilt her so utterly that she imagined that all lovers were like James, and would submit to her quick caprices, her sudden flights. Little she knew Aurelius, who now, with black, bent brows, excited, uncompromising, prepared to show her what he felt.

Felicia wanted everybody, not Aurelius only, but others, to be happy and satisfied. It seemed to her to be almost wicked to sacrifice old and tried friends to the fancies of this new comer.

He had played a part in her life, indeed, but it had been a shadowy part hitherto. Suddenly that shadow had become alive: it spoke for itself; it had a bearing which she could no longer sway at her fancy now. She hardly knew what she felt, or what 'she wanted. Time seemed to her the chief thing that was to explain and harmonise it all, to accustom her to it all. It would be very nice to have him there always, she thought. They might take walks together, and read books together, and little by little he would learn to appreciate her dear, kind Bracys, and they would learn to know him. Suddenly a thought struck her. Could it be Emily Flower who had influenced him against her friends? It was not like him to be so unkind.

Baxter, meanwhile, who had thought that all was explained and clear between them, could not understand these recurring doubts and hesitations. He had made up his mind to come to an issue of some sort; and as he stood behind Felicia's bench he let his fancy drift, as hers had sometimes done —imagined a little scene between them which was to take place in a very few minutes; he was to

speak plainly to her; to the woman who had all
but promised to be his wife; he meant to tell her
how truly he loved her, how unendurable this
present state of suspense had suddenly become.

His whole heart went out to her in tenderness,
and protection. He felt so much and so deeply,
surely she would understand him.

The steamer paddled on its way, the hills floated
past, the people came on board, and struggled off
to shore. . . .

CHAPTER VII.

NO ANSWER.

PRESENTLY, a special peaceful hour of sun and calm content seemed to fall on the travellers: the talk became silenced, the waters deepened, the banks shone more green. Aurelius, looking up, saw that his enemy had allowed herself to be overcome by the stillness, by the tranquil rocking of the boat. She was leaning her head on Miss Harrow's shoulder. Mr. Bracy was at the other end of the boat, claiming acquaintance with a bench full of English people. Jasper was drowsily balancing himself against the bulwark, with both arms widely extended. A swan came sailing out from shore; and then Aurelius began his sentence, and in plain words, not without feeling and honest diffidence, he spoke in a low voice, of which Felicia heard every syllable.

"I have been thinking that I perhaps took you by surprise yesterday," he said. "If it is so you must tell me; you must not be afraid of giving me pain.. Anything is better than want of confidence; but this state of indecision is really more than I

can bear. It was not without painful uncertainty as
to what your answer might be that I came; and yet
you know that my heart is yours, and has been
yours only for all these years. Now whatever your
answer may be, I will abide by it."

Felicia was touched; but she was silent, tapping
her foot against the wooden deck.

"If I had come long ago, perhaps I might have
had more chance," Aurelius went on, frightened by
her silence. "Perhaps you think me presumptuous.
Some one in whom I trust encouraged me to come."

"Emily Flower, I suppose, told you to come,"
said Felicia.

"Yes," stupid Aurelius answered, slowly. "She
told me to come."

Felicia looked away; she did not care to meet
his honest eyes. So he had not come of *himself*,
but only because his cousin had sent him; only
come because he thought she expected it of him.
Her cheek burned with indignant fire.

The little heiress was an autocrat in her way—
in that gentle, vehement, kind-hearted way of hers.
She was an unreasonable autocrat as she sat there
motionless, with her head turned away; her eyes
flashed angrily, but then tears came to put out the
fire. Was no one to be trusted? Did not even
Aurelius love her enough to come straight home to

her. He too, must needs consult, and hesitate, and calculate. James would not have left her all this long time. The steamer paddled on while the two waited in their many voiced silence, but when at last Felicia looked up, the glance that met her own was so sad that she had not the heart to speak the jealous words that had been upon her lips, the crimson died out of her cheeks, her eyes softened. Aurelius took it all so humbly with a sudden hope-lessness that surprised Miss Marlow, who, as I have said, for all her innocent vanities and whimsicalities, did not realise in what estimation Baxter held her. Something touched her. Suddenly her face changed to the old kind face again, she put out her little hand with its soft grey glove.

"We must have our talk another day," she said; "to-morrow, not now. This is not the time."

"No, indeed," said Aurelius, not without em-phasis; for as he spoke Mrs. Bracy was awakening with a wild start and an appealing smile to the company such as reviving sleepers are apt to give. In a minute more she had joined Felicia. Baxter walked away to where Jasper, at his end of the boat, had shifted his spread eagle attitude into one of skewerlike rigidity; while little Mr. Bracy came trotting up panting and bubbling over with informa-tion: "The Alpes, the Alpes," says he; "I'm told

that is the place to go to, Flora; good table d'hôte,
a magnificent view; the divine for you my love, for
us the creature comforts. That family you see sitting near the wheel are going there; the gentleman
strongly recommends the place—a very pleasant,
well-informed person: he was on board the steamer
we crossed in to Calais. I think you would like
him, but of course one can't be sure."

"Edgar," said his wife emphatically, "make what
acquaintances you like, but *pray* do not introduce
them to me. Our party is much too large as it is.
It was a mistake bringing Georgina," she added, as
Felicia looked up at her with a quick glance.

"You did it out of kindness, my love. The poor
girl is thoroughly enjoying herself," cries the little
man, anxiously.

Then all the little bustlings and distractions of
the road come to divert everybody's mind from per-
sonalities.

The travellers by water were turned into passengers by steam, and then again into wretched
fares, wedged side by side in a light red velvet
omnibus, with gilt-looking glasses to reflect their wry
faces. Jasper had more than enough to do grappling
with his parti-coloured bags. Aurelius shouldered
his own small portmanteau and Felicia's dressing-
case, leaving Mr. Bracy, with the help of the amiable

Miss Harrow, to collect the many possessions of his Flora—her writing book (carried loose with her pen and her inkstand), her cushions and sunshades, her luncheon in its basket.

Mrs. Bracy's poet nature invariably required a luncheon basket, the one arm-chair, the most comfortable bed-room, the wing of the chicken, the shady corner in the garden.

The spirit being imprisoned in mortal coil, Flora was wont to say it required absolute freedom from mere temporary discomfort, in order to have full scope to soar.

"So I have observed," says Baxter, dryly, making room for himself among Mrs. Bracy's parasols.

"Ah!" Mrs. Bracy answers, dimly dissatisfied; "you notice everything." I hope my footrest is not in your way.

"For comfort," says Jasper, joining in from the opposite corner of the omnibus, and with a glance at the other passengers, "give me cats to stroke. I thought of bringing a couple abroad, but my uncle dissuaded me."

"Cats!" says Baxter, eying Jasper as if he was a maniac.

But here the omnibus stops at the doors of the hotel; the porters, waiters, majordomos, rush forward breathless, to grip the elbows of the descending travellers.

5*

CHAPTER VIII.

BY A FOUNTAIN.

IT is very hot and sultry in the hotel garden. The fountain and the piano from the saloon are playing a duett. The fountain itself must be boiling after the morning's glare, but the sound of the water is not the less delightful to parched ears. An old man sits on a bench by a charming and handsome young woman; a grandchild is playing at his feet. The old man's is a world-known name; he has swayed nations and armies in his life, but he is quietly stirring his coffee in the shadow of the chestnut tree. Presently, obsequiosity in thread gloves, with a newspaper in its hand, comes up, bows low, and takes a respectful chair at the old diplomat's invitation. Felicia is sitting in a little arbour close by, leaning back half asleep, and swinging her little feet. She has taken off her felt hat, and pushed back the two plaits that usually make a sort of coronet about her pretty head. The diamond ornament at her throat glistens like the radiating lights of the fountain; the folds of her China silk dress

shine with tints that come and go. She is in a
peaceful, expectant state of mind, drowsy, prepared
for happiness to come to her; it is much too sultry
weather to go in search of it. "How can Georgina
go on practising as she does through the heat of the
day?" Meanwhile, Miss Harrow, the musician, leaves
off for an instant, looks up at the approach of Colonel
Baxter, or answers when he asks her whether she
has seen Miss Marlow, "Yes, Colonel Baxter, you
will find her by the fountain;" and then she begins
again with fresh spirit, and some vague and re-
animating sense of an audience. The dry knobbly
fingers rattle on, her bony head nods in time, her
skinny kid feet beat upon the pedal with careful
attention. It would be difficult to say of what use
Georgina's monotonous music is to herself, or to art,
or to the world in general; but she does her best,
while Felicia by the fountain shrugs her pretty
shoulders. Miss Marlow is still sleepily watching
the old diplomat and his coffee-pot under the tree,
and then her soft, heavy eyes travel on to the end
of the terrace, where she can see the line of the
mountains. Everything to-day is sleepy, and heaped
with shadows and tranquil languor. The blue is
kindling beyond the line of crests, the lovely azure
flows from peak to peak, from pass and glacier to
rocky summit; the sky seems to catch fire as Felicia

looks, and a white *something* leaps to meet it. The
bushes about are all in flower; a whole parterre of
olive-green and starry constellations is scenting the
air. How hot, how still it is! how straight the paths
look, just crossed here and there by some faint
shadow! One's life seems passed, Fay thinks, in
straggling from shadow into sunshine, and from
sunshine into shadow again. Outside the low wall
the people go passing—the prim young German
ladies with their tight waists, slightly lame from their
clumsy high heels; the little fat Englishman, conscious of his puggaree; the Swiss family, in drab,
with hand-bags to match, each shaded by a dome
of grey calico. Then Felicia vacantly stares at the
shining ball upon its stick, growing in front of the
hotel, and which reflects the sun and the human
beings coming and going upon the face of the earth,
all gradually curved: and while she is still looking
—the figures issue from the ball, they turn into
well-known faces and forms; one sits down beside
her on the bench, another holds out with both hands
a china plate, which breaks into a star. Felicia's
little head falls gently back upon a branch of myrtle.
She is asleep, and peacefully slumbering in the
valley of ease, with a sweet childish face, breathing
softly; and Aurelius, black and determined, who has
come to reproach her, to insist upon an explanation,

stands watching her slumbers for a moment. As he watches his face softens and melts, and then he walks away very quietly. When Felicia awoke with a start about an hour later, she found a soft knitted shawl thrown over her. Baxter did not appear again till dinner time, and during dinner he said nothing particular, looked nothing remarkable. He sat next Felicia, attended to her wants, and talked very pleasantly in the intervals.

The Bracys were bent upon enjoying the various pleasures of the place; and Mr. Bracy, having learned from the head waiter next day that a band played in the gardens of the establishment from four to five, urged his ladies to attend the entertainment. They consented somewhat lazily, for, as I have said, the weather was hot, and exertion seemed unwelcome, but once they were there it was pleasant enough — a little breeze came rustling over their heads; the company sat chattering, turning over newspapers, eating ices; the tunes were dinning gaily; cigars were puffing; friends were greeting. Felicia was sitting between Mr. Bracy and Miss Harrow, under the shade of an awning, Mrs. Bracy was taking a turn on Jasper's indigo arm, when Mr. Bracy suddenly started up to greet some of his numerous steam-boat acquaintances, and at the same minute somebody came striding over a low iron fence at the back of Felicia's chair, and sat down beside her, in Mr. Bracy's vacant place. I need not say that this was Baxter, who had chosen his time.

"We can have our talk now, Felicia. You gave me no chance last night. Miss Harrow, would you kindly leave us for a few minutes?" (Georgina instantly vanished in discreet alarm, notwithstanding Felicia's imploring glances), and then Baxter went on very quietly, but with increasing emphasis: "You *must* face the truth, Felicia; you must give me my answer. Ask no one else to advise you—tell me what you wish from yourself! This much I have a right to ask. I have kept out of your way all to-day on purpose; now you must let me speak plainly. All night long I lay awake wondering what you would decide. I know," he added, that as far as the world goes I am about as bad a match as you could make, but I don't think anyone could ever love you better."

She heard his voice break a little as he spoke, and then he waited for the last time in renewed emotion for the answer that was to decide both their fates. He was really not asking too much. As he said, he had a right to an answer. Was it some evil demon that prompted Felicia? She meant to spare him, as she thought, to gain time for herself.

"Why are you always thinking of my money?"
she said. "Mrs. Bracy tells me it can all be tied
up if I marry; it need not concern you."

Her words somehow jarred upon Baxter; indeed,
they jarred upon Felicia herself as she spoke them.
He was over-wrought, perhaps unreasonable, in his
excitement.

"It is you and Mrs. Bracy, not I, who are always
thinking about money," he cried. "If you can
suspect me of such unworthy motives, you are not
the woman I took you for. Felicia, trust me—make
no conditions——"

She laid her hand upon his arm to quiet him,
but he went on all the more vehemently. "You let
their flatteries poison your true self. I will agree to
none of their bargains. If you love me, marry me
with your heart and with all that you have. If you
do not care for me, send me away, and I will
certainly trouble you no longer. Oh, Felicia! you
should not use me so."

He spoke in a voice which frightened her, with
a sort of reproachful despotism that startled and
terrified Miss Marlow far more than he had any idea
of. When she answered, it was to a sudden scraping of fiddles, to which she unconsciously raised her
tones.

"I cannot see what you have to complain of,"

she said, trembling. "If you insist upon only marrying me with my money, I certainly cannot agree to
the bargain. As I told Mrs. Bracy, I do not grudge
you the money; if you wanted some I would give
you some, but not myself with it. You——"

"Felicia!" He started up, and spoke in a cold
rasping voice. "You need not have insulted me.
You are ruined by your miserable fortune. My
truths don't suit you—their lies please you better.
Good-bye; be happy your own way with the companions you prefer." You have given me my
answer.

"Colonel Baxter!" cried Felicia, starting up too,
as he turned. "Don't go, you know you promised
to come with us to-morrow."

Aurelius looked her hard in the face, with his
dark reproachful angry eyes. "I could only have
come in one way," he said; "that is over for ever."

"For—for ever," Felicia faltered, dropping back
into her chair again, for he was gone. The musicians
had ended, the whole place seemed suddenly empty
and astir, a crowd seemed to surround her, she
thought once that Baxter had returned, but it was
only Jasper standing beside her. "I came back to
look for you," said he. "Aunt Flora is gone to the
hotel. What is this?" and he suddenly stooped and
picked up a dirty little bit of yellow rag that was

hanging to one of the railings. "See what quality! What exquisite modulations of tone!" cries Jasper, holding his prize up in the air.

"Exquisite," said Felicia, mechanically—she knew not to what, nor did she look at the precious rag. At the first opportunity she escaped from him, and ran upstairs and along the passage that led to her own room. Once there, she locked the door, still in a sort of maze. She sat stupidly upon the red velvet sofa, staring through the window at the great white Jungfrau, which seemed to stare back at her. What had she done? Had she been wise—had she been acting with sense and judgment and sincerity? There are passes in life where it is scarcely possible to realise very clearly the names of the various impulses by which we are driven. Every moment brings a fresh impression, a fresh aspect of things. Each impression is true but partial, each aspect is sincere but incomplete. Perhaps at such times the only clue is the dim sense of a whole to be completed, the craving for more time, for distance that defines, and cancels the less important facts, and reveals the truth. Felicia had followed her impulse and let Aurelius go, though in her heart she would fain have called him back to her again. Baxter had set the estimation of others beyond his own conviction. Instead of thinking only of Felicia, he had thought of his shortcomings; and she, instead of thinking of Baxter, had talked about him to Flora Bracy. It had all been so short that she could scarcely realise it. If her happiness had been vague, her unhappiness was still more intangible. What had these two days brought about? A possibility. Aurelius had reproached her, she had answered angrily; but it was all over. "For ever," he had said. She sat there till the loud dinner-bell began to din through the house, and raps at the door reminded her that Pringle was outside, the others were waiting. Could she bear to tell them? Some feeling in her heart shrank from their comments. She felt that it would be best to try and behave as if nothing had happened. She bathed her aching head, let Pringle smooth her hair and then hurried down stairs.

CHAPTER IX.

TABLE D'HOTE.

ALL the doors were opening and the tenants coming out of their rooms, with various appetites and attempts at adornment. Mrs. Bracy was arrayed in her most gorgeous hues, with an Indian scarf wound about her ample shoulders; but even Mrs. Bracy's colours faded before some of the amazing rainbows that appeared balanced on their high heels, puffed, frizzed, stuffed out with horsehair, tied in by strings, and dabbed with red and yellow, as, male and female, they descended the great staircase and took their places at the long table. Felicia's place was, as usual, by Jasper and Mrs. Bracy. Miss Harrow sat opposite with Mr. Bracy. The day before Baxter had been at Felicia's right hand, and all dinner time they had chatted comfortably together. To-day she looked round at his empty place; it was filled by a well-worn foreign edition of Miss Harrow, a little haggard woman, with an anxious glance and appetite, who seemed to eat not because she was hungry, but because she had paid for her dinner, and was determined to have her money's worth. She looked at Miss Marlow once or twice. "They will give you ice if you demand them," she said, in tolerable English, to Felicia; "and you have a right to a wing of the chick. Some people have left since yesterday; you have been moved up by Mr. Franz. You are not such a large party as you were. I am all alone! yes, I am always travelling alone. Where is that gentleman who was travelling with you yesterday?"

Felicia felt her cheeks blush up suddenly, and then she blushed again with vexation.

"Interlaken is a dull place for gentlemen who can valk. Ah! here comes the salad," said the little woman, who saw it all, but pretended to be looking at her plate. "Do not pass it over. Mr. Franz makes such good salad. I tell the lady what good salad you make," said she to the head waiter; and then the little ghost-like woman began to devour the green lettuce, in a curious hurried way, as if she feared that her food might be taken away from her. "It is sad to be all alone in places like these," she went on, with a quick look at Felicia. "I make friends, but people go away, and it is all to begin again;" and she flirted out a great green fan, and began to whisk it backwards and forwards.

The great hall grew hotter and hotter, the voices

seemed to rise, the clatter to increase, the waiters
were flying about, a moraine of smoking dishes, of
plates, and scraps of comestibles seemed hurled by
some invisible means across the great counter at the
far end of the room. Felicia's spirits sank lower
and lower. All alone! Something in the woman's
voice seemed to rouse a dismal echo in her own
mind; the sight of that thin nervous hand, flickering,
darting at the salt, flying at the dishes, in the place
of Aurelius's tranquil neighbourhood, seemed to play
upon every nerve. Where was he? What was he
thinking? Would that poor woman never keep
quiet? She had a longing to seize the skinny hand
and tie it down. If Felicia disliked her unknown
companion's eager movements, the firm grasp of Mrs.
Bracy's fat familiar fingers was almost as trying.

"Do not talk so much to that horrid woman,"
said the poetess. "She wants to join on to our
party. I will not have her impose upon us."

"Hush—she will hear you," says Felicia; for she
saw the little bat-like lady's eyes fixed upon Mrs.
Bracy's lips.

"My dear child, these people have no conscience,"
said Flora, crossly. "Edgar," bending forward, "what
do you say?"

"We shall have Fine Weather for our Expedition
To-morrow!" shouts Mr. Bracy, across the table.

"This gentleman," pointing to a very red face and a flannel shirt, "has come just from Mürren, by the Scheideck. He tells me the mountains are looking remarkable fine just now. Who knows what inspirations, eh, Flora, my love?" and Mr. Bracy suddenly began something confidentially, in an undertone, to his new-found friend, and Felicia could tell from the expression of the little man's eyebrows that he was speaking of the Poems. Then her thoughts travelled away from the clatter of the present to the mountains of to-morrow. She impatiently longed to get to them, to breathe their silent pure air, to escape this stifling valley, which had suddenly lost all interest for her, all vitality. Her heart sank, and sank into some depth, where pain began and no happiness could reach. What was Jasper saying? did she feel faint? would she come out? A sort of mist fell between her and her neighbours.

"Take my fan," says the strange lady.

Mrs. Bracy looked at her young companion, and thought of proposing to leave the table with her, but the ices were coming round at that moment; they looked so refreshing in their pink pyramids that, on second thoughts, she helped herself largely. "This will do you good, dear Felicia," she said; but Felicia jumped up quickly, and escaped through a door which happened to be behind her chair. They found her sitting quietly on the balcony outside their sitting-room, when they rejoined her. She looked very pale; she was watching the floating snow-range in its evening dream of light and silver and faint azalea tints. Others had come out to see the wonders of that sunset.

The tongues of fire fell that night upon the company assembled in the garden of the Hôtel des Alpes at Interlaken—Parthians, with many glances and chignons; clergymen and Jews and infidels taking their hard-earned holidays together; the light fell upon them all, and they all spoke in words of wondering praise.

The very children seemed impressed. The fire leapt from snow to snow, dazzling in tender might. The mountain seemed to put out great wings, to tremble with a mysterious life; the snow-fields hung mid-air, the radiance of their summits seemed to spread into space. People came out from the long tables where they had been dining, streaming out into the garden where the miracle was to be seen. Voices changed, people changed; for a few moments one impulse seemed to touch all these human beings, calling them to something most mysterious and beyond them, utterly beyond expression or remembrance. Such a mood coming from without, im-

posed by inanimate things upon the living, seems to
be like some ancient history of revelation realised
once again. The faces shone as they turned towards the mountains all burning in their light.

Upon a balcony of the hotel our Poetess had
appeared shrouded in a long gauze veil. She stood,
tablets in hand, and pausing for inspiration. Mrs.
Bracy hated people to talk when she was taking
notes. She desired some one, who exclaimed in the
room within, to be silent now, and presently her
own voice was the only one to be heard upraised
in shrill approbation of the solemn beauty of the
evening.

One or two people had left the garden and the
crowd, and crossed the road and sat quietly upon
the low parapet opposite, watching. The Swiss
women, who seem hired at so much a day to walk
slowly up and down the avenue, in starched sleeves,
with go-carts, ceased to drag for a moment and
stopped to look. So did the sentimental German
ladies with their hand-bags, and the eager English
tourists, and the Swiss students in spectacles, with
their arms full of books, and the Russian and
American travellers in their well-fitting clothes.

The glory passed on by degrees; an awful shadow
rose from the valley and mounted upward, rapid,
remorseless. The beautiful flames of a moment sank

away; the pinnacles still dominated with their fiery points—an instant more and all was over in that wonder-world, and the oil-lamps resumed the reign upon earth.

The old diplomat on his terrace went back to his evening paper; two young girls at a window clasped each other's hands in youthful enthusiasm and regret; the lady in the balcony continued her remarks.

"Did you not observe the marvellous effect of that last, last tint, succumbing as it were to the great——"

"It is a passion of atmospheric word painting," interrupted Jasper, who had been hastily making a sketch with some yellow ochre and carmine.

There was a sudden burst of voices from the garden below. "Sugar, absolutely like sugar!" cried a young Russian lady to her partner of the night before.

"Sugar!" exclaims Mrs. Bracy in a sepulchral voice; "do they liken that noble mass to sugar—that livid, living, loving——"

"My dear Flora, do see after Miss Marlow!" said little Mr. Bracy, anxiously.

"It is nothing, nothing," Felicia whispers, trying in vain to hush her sobs. Suddenly the poor little thing had burst into tears, and all the gold stoppers

out of her travelling-bag were produced in vain to
soothe her troubles. Some remembrance of the
night before had come over her, some sudden realisation of her lonely state, and yet Baxter was only ten
miles off, toiling up the mountain road to Grindelwald, as it lies on the mountain side, at the foot of
the Eiger, and of the great Wetterhorn, with its
crown of floating mist.

It had been so sudden, she could scarcely believe in it. Baxter was gone—no one but herself
seemed to miss him. Why was he not there to see
the beautiful sunset? If her brief happiness had
been vague, her present unhappiness seemed still
more intangible. Aurelius had been unkind, unreasonable; she had answered unkindly—that was
all, and everything was changed somehow, and why
was she so miserable?

Mrs. Bracy may have had her suspicions, but
she bided her time, and kept her words to herself.
Felicia was petted, sent to bed, to all sorts of vague
agitated dreams of parting and desolate places, to
dreary startings and remorseful awakenings, as the
night sped on with stars without, to the murmurs,
and muffled cries from the valley.

And then, after the long night came morning,
as it comes, with a sort of surprise; day breaking
once more after the darkness of many hours; the

sweet irresistible light reaching everywhere — into every corner — spreading across the valleys as they lie dimly in their dreams. It starts along the mountain side, the shadows melt, disperse. Crisp ridges come into streaming relief; then the snow fields are gained, and lo! mysterious, simultaneous, behold the lights break forth on every side, and the dazzling white Jungfrau floats dominant once more.

CHAPTER X.

AN OFFER OF MARRIAGE.

They set off for Grindelwald next day in two quick trotting carriages. The horses were hung with cheerful little bells, and seemed well able to face the steep pass. "How delicious!" cried Felicia, as the wheels of her einspanner rolled across the resounding boards of a wooden bridge. The young lady leant forward eagerly, and the cool breeze from the torrent came blowing into her blushing face. She looked down with bright-eyed wonder at the foaming water rushing underneath.

"Look! mem," said Pringle; "what a picture!" And so it was, for the snow-capped mountain-heads uprose at the turn of the winding road; the grey river was eddying on its way, and the charcoal-burners had lit a fire that flamed down among the boulders by the running stream.

It was almost evening when they reached their journey's end; coming up through the village street, with its busy little shops lighting up, and the friendly clusters of peasant folk gossiping after their day's

work. The great mountains actually overhung the
little village; huge rocks reared their mighty sides,
all lined and seamed with the intricate net-work of
delicate shadow; the pale white crests clustered beyond the rocks. Felicia was almost overpowered
by the pomp and stately splendour of this mighty
Court, to which she was not yet accustomed. She
could hardly tear herself away from the terrace in
front of the windows.

"Dinner, ladies, dinner!" cried Mr. Bracy, calling
from the dining-room of the hotel. As they came
in, he made them take their places, talking as usual,
while he saw to everybody's requirements. He had
just seen their friend Colonel Baxter's name in the
book. "He slept here last night, and has gone on
to the upper glacier," says Mr. Bracy, sharpening his
knife.

Jasper had also seen the Colonel's departure, not
without satisfaction. He had been cross-questioning
Georgina in the einspanner coming up.

"There was something," Georgina owned confidentially. "They had a long, long conversation. I
think she is angry."

"She wants a protector," said Jasper thoughtfully,
twirling the silver ring upon his first finger.

I think the same evil imp which so maliciously
prompted Felicia now involved the unfortunate

painter in his toils, and began to whisper to him that Aurelius being gone, Jasper's own hour had come. It was for him to make Felicia forget the faithless Colonel. No one knew for certain what had happened; only that Felicia was changed and preoccupied was evident to them all. Jasper ate his dinner as usual, but ostentatiously drank a great deal of wine. He began to turn sentimental; from sentimental art to artistic sentiment the step is but short.

The next day was Sunday. The bell of the village church had been going for an hour before Felicia arose; as she dressed she had peeped out of her window at the figures passing up the street, quiet and collected, in their smart Sunday coiffes and beavers. As for the English, they also put on their best bonnets, and assembled in the dining-room of the hotel where in those days the English service was held once a week. The tables were rolled out of the way, the plates were put inside the wooden dresser, the chairs were set out in three rows, the blinds drawn half-way down, and a few straggling travellers came into the room where the usual traffic was for a time suspended.

But it was impossible not to feel the incongruity of the form in which much had been expressed that seemed almost incompatible with the associations of

the place and its appurtenances. As the congregation left the room, the waiters began clattering their
knives and forks and spreading the dinner tables
once more; and Felicia walked away, glad to escape
up the village street towards the little churchyard,
across which came the strain of a hymn sung by
many voices.

Felicia went to the door and looked into the
quiet old building, where she saw a great number
of the villagers assembled, each in their places. The
brown-coated men were on one side, and the women
were sitting in rows along the other aisle; the old
ones in their coiffes, the young ones with their pretty
brown braids tied with velvet, displaying clean white
sleeves and black bodices. The preacher was ascending his pulpit. It was all very quiet and de-
corous. The very bareness of the old church seemed
to be more impressive than any tawdry ornament.
She listened, but she could scarcely follow the
German of the preacher, and so she walked on a
little way, turning one thing and another over in
her mind. She came presently to a narrow bridge
across a stream, and she stood looking thoughtfully
down at the rushing water. Where was she travelling to? Among what past and present things was
she living? She started hearing a step. No; it was
only Jasper in his indigo suit.

It was Jasper, who came up to her, and suddenly, to Felicia's dismay, began a long and desultory speech in which figured gem-like flames of twin lives, rosy raptures of love-greeting, and double stars encircling their own progression. Miss Marlow might not have understood a word he said, or that he intended this as a serious proposal, had not the unlucky youth seized her by the hand and suddenly attempted to thrust the large silver ring which he usually wore on to her finger. Felicia fairly lost her temper, and snatched her hand away. The ring flashed into the stream. What! she had parted from the only man she had ever cared for in order to be insulted by this absurd and ridiculous mockery! It seemed like a judgment upon her, a mockery of fate. "The companions you have chosen!" she seemed to hear Aurelius' voice saying. What would he say if he were there now? She seemed to see the reproachful look of his eyes there before her.

"How dare you ask me to marry you?" she cried to poor astonished Jasper, "when you know you do not care for me one bit? Do you know I might have married someone who has loved me for years if I had not been ill advised, if I had not been a fool and thrown away my best chance? And do you suppose I should think of marrying you," cried Felicia, "who do not care for me, and for whom I do not care?" and she turned and began hurrying back through a shower of rain towards the hotel. Jasper must have been possessed; he followed her step by step, protesting in the language of a troubadour rather than that of a reasonable being. They had reached the churchyard by this time. "Do leave me," cried Felicia, stopping short. "Don't you see I want you to go?" and as she spoke she stamped her foot in a fit of most unladylike passion, then as suddenly burst into tears. The good old preacher's voice had been droning on peaceably all this while inside the church, and Felicia's explanations might have been continued even more fully if the sermon had not suddenly come to an end, and the congregation issued forth, opening its umbrellas, walking off with short sturdy legs, tucking up its ample petticoats and trousers. The men, in their brown coats and clumsy boots, looked like good-natured bears trotting down the wet road; the women, with their kind faces, and quaint lace snoods, were like figures out of some long-forgotten dream. They passed on, quietly streaming down the street; some took to the fields, but more of them were going straight from the service to their Sunday gathering at the tavern by the bridge. Disconcerted Jasper marched off with the crowd, leaving Felicia to get home as best she could. She found him, however, waiting for her at the entrance of the hotel.

"I'm afraid I carried off the umbrella," he said, with an uneasy laugh. "I've waited to tell you that —er," here he looked very red and foolish, "you quite misunderstood me, Miss Marlow. You didn't do me justice, indeed you didn't. This shall make no difference on my part, and I hope you will keep a fellow's confidence sacred."

"I have certainly no wish to repeat what has happened," said Felicia, still unrelenting.

"I shall start early to-morrow," said Jasper, irritated. "After a day alone in the mountains I shall know how to master my feelings. Perhaps if I meet Colonel Baxter," he added, "you would like me to send him down."

This was said with a mixture of feminine spite and masculine jealousy. He felt he had revenged himself on Miss Marlow. Felicia did not answer; she looked Jasper full in the face, and swept past him haughtily to her own room. Poor Felicia! she began to find her circumstances somewhat trying. Mrs. Bracy was especially snappish that evening; Georgina looked tearful and reproachful. Miss Marlow wondered whether Jasper had kept his own sacred confidence. It was quite a relief when kind little

Mr. Bracy bustled in with a guide and a programme for the following day.

"What do you say to seeing something of the environs? We might all start off to meet our artist to-morrow on his return? We can lunch at the châlet at the entrance to the upper glacier — excellent cookery, I am told; fine view of the mountains. Suit you? eh, Flora, my love?"

Flora answered severely that she certainly should not go, she needed repose. Then she added, with intention: "Probably Felicia would also wish to remain behind?"

Nothing was farther from Felicia's wish. She merely said she would like to see the upper glacier. Three mules were accordingly ordered, with three guides to match. The mules were in the stables, the guides were spinning like teetotums with their mountain maidens in the ball-room.

———

CHAPTER XI.

CLIMBING UP.

They were all somewhat late in their start next morning. At last they got off, the ladies in their improvised skirts, Mr. Bracy trotting faithfully by their side in knickerbockers, and with an ice-axe which he had borrowed, but which he found some difficulty in managing. After passing the church and the village, and crossing the stream of provoking associations, the way led up a narrow ledge cut along the side of the rock. The path rose abruptly, and the great plain seemed to sink away at their feet. The mules stumbled on steadily; and, after some half-hour's arid climb, the path, with a sudden turn, led into a burst of gentle green and shade and sweetness. Mosses overflowed the huge granite stones; streams rippled; the flowers which were over down below still starred white among the rocks; ferns started from the cracks in the huge fallen masses; the path wound and straggled on across meadows into woods of fragrant pine, flowing green and flowering light, until at last the travellers reached a wide green alp, covered with herds of browsing cattle, open to the clouds, and clothed with exquisite verdure and silence.

There is a little erection built at the summit of the great alp for travellers to rest, and to eat wild strawberries if they will, provided by the villagers, while they admire the noble prospect. Felicia dismounted here, and went on a little way a-head into a wood of mountain ash and birch and chestnut. It seemed enchanted to her; so were the tree stems, and so was the emerald turf, still sparkling with the heavy morning dew. Every leaf seemed quivering with life. This sweet abundance lay on every side, tender little stems, bearing their burden of seed or flower; leaves veined and gilt and bronzed. The eyebright, with its gentle velvet marks, sparkled among the roots of the trees; moneywort flung its golden flowers; grass of parnassus lit its silver stars. Everything was delicate and tender in fragrant beauty. A little higher up Felicia could see the crimson berries, growing among grey stones and hairy mosses and pine roots. The leaves were like gold, the fruit glowing like rubies. A little peasant girl was climbing down the bank with a bunch of late wood strawberries. The child's little fingers seemed the only ones that should pluck such fairy work. Felicia took the bunch of crimson fruit, and

gave the little girl not money but a little chain of
beads she happened to wear on her wrist. The
child clapped her hands and ran away as hard as
her little legs could carry her. Then came the
mules and the guides, climbing up the road from
the châlet, and the cavalcade set forth once more.

High up at the end of a long winding mountain
pass stands a little châlet, where cutlets are grilling,
guides sit sipping their wine and cracking their
jokes in the kitchen. The parlour, with its wooden
walls, wooden tables and benches, is filled by cara-
vans of travellers; some are on their way to the
glacier, others are returning home; everybody is
more or less excited, exhausted, hungry, discursive.
The wooden hut echoes with voices, with the clatter
of steel upon earthenware. Sometimes, as the kitchen
door swings upon its hinges, the guides begin a sort
of jodelling chorus; sometimes an impatient horse
strikes up a snorting and pawing on the platform
outside. From the terrace itself you may look across
a great icy abyss to the mountains rising silent and
supreme; but the châlet is a little commonplace
noisy human oasis, hanging among the great natural
solemnities all about, mighty rocks striking their
shadows age after age, deserted seas that seem to
have been frozen as they tossed their unquiet waves
in vast curves against the summer sky; a wide valley

blinked at by our wondering eyes, as we try to name this or that glittering point. Someone fires off an old blunderbuss, and the echo bangs down among the rocky clefts, striking and reverberating; and then perhaps the host comes out courteously to announce that our portion of bread and cheese is served, and hungry travellers forget echoes, fatigue, and wonder in the absorbing process of luncheon. The German party were enjoying potato soup, and shouting over their dish as the ladies entered.

"Here is our table," says Mr. Bracy. "Kalb-flesh, hey! I hope you ladies are not tired of veal cutlets." Then, lowering his voice, "Our friend from Berne. I knew him at once—very much altered, poor man—sadly burnt by the sun. Has been through a great deal of fatigue since we last saw him."

Felicia looked, and could scarcely recognise their fellow-traveller, so scorched and seamed, so ripped and hacked was he. His lips were swelled, his eyes were crimson, his wild tumbled hair hung limp about his face, his neat tight-fitting clothes were torn and soiled, and burst out at knees and elbows; his enamelled shirt-collar alone remained intact, except that a glittering crack in one place showed the steel; a more forlorn object it would be difficult to imagine. He himself, however, seemed

well satisfied with his appearance, and with adven-
tures, even more colossal than he had hoped for.
He had lost his way up among the rocks the evening before, having scrambled up to see the sunset.
Then came the darkness. He had been able to
descend only by the most desperate heroism.

"He was a madman to put himself into such a
situation," said the host, confidentially, to Miss Marlow, as he dusted her plate and wiped a glass which
he set before her. "I discovered him by chance;
half an hour later, it would have been too late—we
could have done nothing. I sent our man off to
help him across the glacier. The Herr saw him
coming, and called out, 'Have you food?' Peter,
our man, said, 'Yes; I have veal you can eat, and
gain strength to return.' He came back quite exhausted, and has been drinking all day to refresh
himself. Travellers should not go into such places
without guides; they get themselves into trouble,
and we are blamed. Only this morning two gentlemen set out alone; one had spent the night here,
an English colonel. The other arrived from Grindelwald. I said to him, 'Take Peter to show you the way
to the upper glacier.' Not he. But it is not safe."

"Which way did they go?" said Felicia, putting
down her knife and fork, and looking up into the
host's weather-beaten face.

"How can I tell?" said he, "or where they may be now!"

"It couldn't be Jasper," said Mr. Bracy, rather anxiously; "he wouldn't have done anything rash. Just ask the man what sort of traveller it was, my dear."

"One was black and somewhat silent," said the host; "military bear-like."

"That couldn't have been Jasper," said Mr. Bracy, relieved.

"And the other?" said Miss Harrow.

"The second," said the man doubtfully, "he was strangely dressed; he wore a feather, and seemed somewhat out of the common, an actor, perhaps, large ears, like Peter's yonder."

Felicia hoped that Mr. Bracy did not understand, and hastily asked whether they had not written their names in the travellers' book; and sure enough, there upon the long page were the two signatures, Jasper's curling J's and Baxter's close writing. "Jasper is sure to be back," said Mr. Bracy, slightly disquieted still; "he is very careful about keeping people waiting, his aunt has taught him punctuality. He has gone sketching somewhere, or forgotten the time. Of course I don't know anything about the Colonel. Very odd of him, wasn't it, to leave us as he did without a word?"

7*

"Very odd," said Felicia, faltering a little. They sat over luncheon as long as they could, and then ordered up coffee to pass the time; and then Felicia left the other two, and went in front and stood gazing at the great hopeless wall of mountains.

"You don't mind waiting a little for him?" said little Mr. Bracy, fussing up presently. "It is getting rather late, but I'm afraid my wife might be anxious if we went back without the boy. There's a nice bench this way and an excellent telescope, one of Casella's, if you wish to look through; excellent maker, you know." Felicia eagerly accepted Mr. Bracy's suggestion. Was it some faint hope that Baxter might return? Was it anxiety for Jasper that made her so reluctant to leave the place? Not long after Mr. Bracy disappeared, again to reappear in excellent spirits. A party had just arrived—two American gentlemen and their guide. They brought news of Jasper. They had passed an artist sketching the crevasses under an umbrella, not very far off, at the entrance of the glacier.

"It must have been Jasper," says Mr. Bracy; "poor dear fellow, how hard he works. I must say I wish he would come down. I have a great mind to go a little way to look for him, if you two girls don't mind being left." Felicia assured Mr. Bracy

that she had no objection whatever to being left,
and in truth drew a great breath of relief when she
found herself at last alone. But it was only for a
minute; then the host came up and asked her to
look through his glass, and Felicia, not liking to
refuse, did as he directed and peeped through the
long brass tube. At first everything looked blurred
and indistinct, but a good deal of shifting and turning dispelled the clouds by degrees, then clearer
and well-defined images grew out of the confused
floating visions that had bewildered her at first.
Then little by little she became absorbed in this
new wonder-world into which she had come as by a
miracle; she forgot the stage on which she stood;
she heeded not the confusion of sounds round about
her as she gazed, every moment more and more absorbed, into the spirit of that awful silence and
snowy vastness which seemed to spread before her.
She seemed carried away on unknown wings into
vast regions undreamt of hitherto, past snowy cavities,
by interminable gorges haunted by terrible shrouded
figures trailing their stiff grave clothes, and bending
in an awful procession. Then came great fields of
glittering virgin snow blazing in the sun, then perhaps a narrow track stitched by human footsteps,
curiously discernible. Felicia could follow the line
for a while, then she lost it, and again it would

reappear ever ascending, to the foot of a great gulley where all traces seemed lost. . . .

"How absorbed you are!" said Georgina's voice at her ear. "Can you make anything out? May I have a look?" Felicia did not answer. She was trembling convulsively; then she suddenly seized the other woman's wrist in a tight clutch. "I see something. Oh Georgina, for heaven's sake look, and tell me what you see." But Georgina looking shifted the great glass and could not adjust it again. Felicia, wildly wringing her hands, began to call for a guide, for anyone who knew. "I saw a man hanging to a rock, a tremendous rock," she said. The guides and the host all came up in some excitement, and eye after eye was applied. "You see the track, follow the track lower down, lower down," cried Miss Marlow. "Do you see nothing?" and then when none could find the place, she pushed the last comer away and with trembling hands followed again the tiny thread she had discovered, recalling each jutting peak and form, and there was the great rock shining in the sun, but the man was there no longer. "I saw him, I tell you," she cried, "he is killed, he has fallen. Oh Georgina, it may have been Colonel Baxter!" and she stamped in an agony of terror. Georgina with pale lips faltered something. The guides tried to reassure the ladies. It

may have been fancy, people often were mistaken.
'I tell you I saw him slip," cried Felicia, and old
Johann, an experienced guide, looked, paused, and
looked again. "It is a nasty place," said he, looking puzzled. "It was close by there that we met
the Englishman with his paint-box. That is our
track the lady has been following, but there is another beside it. I cannot venture to say she is mistaken." Felicia's conviction seemed to have spread
to the guides. They examined the track again and
again, and began talking the matter over. Two of
them presently came forward, looking grave, and
proposed that they should go off then and there,
and see if there was anything to be done. · "It is
like last night's experience over again," said the
host; "the sun will be setting in a couple of hours;
you must take lanterns if you go, for you won't be
back by daylight, and what can you do, if so be
the man has fallen? What did I say about people's
foolhardiness?" he continued, turning to Georgina.
"Your papa has taken Peter our man with him, that
is something reasonable. If this is one of the English travellers I told you of who went off alone, it
will show you that I do not speak without thinking."

. Poor Mr. Bracy came back with Peter in another ·
hour to share the general consternation. His first

words were to enquire if Jasper had returned, and then he was told what had occurred. He kept up with great courage before the girls, declaring all would be well, but his looks belied his words. His face was pale and drawn; the poor little man stood with one helpless eye applied to the telescope long after the darkness had fallen, and it was impossible to distinguish any object at three yards' distance.

Felicia's secret fears were for Baxter, though the others maintained that it must have been Jasper she had seen. As the hours went on and the painter did not return, it seemed more and more likely that they were right. Baxter was safe enough, if she had but known it. He had not even been alone. He had been all day with the guide whom he had appointed to meet him. It was indeed poor Jasper whose peril had been revealed in that horrible minute.

Baxter was quietly returning with his friend Melchior, the guide, from a long day's walk in the snow, when he happened to see Jasper sitting at his easel perched on a rock, and sketching the surrounding abyss.

"There is a man I wish to avoid," said the Colonel to his guide, and the man laughed, and proposed that they should make a short circuit and

come back to the track just below the place where
the painter was at work.

Jasper had not returned to luncheon on purpose;
he happened to have sandwiches in his pocket, and
he wished to cause some slight anxiety. Now that
the light was beginning to fail, he began to feel the
want of his dinner; but a fancy seized him to climb
a huge rock that rose abruptly behind him, and to
get one last view of the surrounding country before
going down. He had left his easel but a few yards
behind him, he climbed a steep crag with great
agility, and with some exertion he got round a sharp
protruding block, which led, as he thought, to a
little rocky platform, when suddenly his foot slipped.
He had fallen but a little way, he righted himself
with difficulty, and then slipped again. Jasper was
frightened and completely sobered, perhaps for the
first time in his life.

There was no one looking on. There were a
few rocks and pine trees down below; overhead the
great crags were fading from moment to moment
into more terrible impassivity. He could scarcely
imagine how he had ever reached his present perilous position. Was it he himself, Jasper Bracy, who
was here alone and clinging desperately—was it for
life?—to the face of this granite boulder? What would
they all say at home if they knew of his position?

He could not face the thought, for he had a heart for all his vagaries. He seemed to realise it all so suddenly—his aunt's exclamations, his uncle's wistful face came before him. "And poor Georgina," thought Jasper.

All this did not take long to pass through his mind as he clung desperately to the ledge on to which he had come; even to an experienced mountaineer it would have been an ugly pass. The rocks were hard as iron, worn smooth by a glacier; there seemed neither foot nor cranny to get on to; the evening was fast approaching: there was no chance of anyone descrying him from the distant châlet.

Jasper tried to say his prayers, poor boy; but he could not think of anything but the burning pain in his hands and back, the choking breath which seemed so terrible: his head swam, he knew that the end was at hand, he could hold on no longer. Perhaps five minutes had passed since he fell, but what a five minutes, blotting out the whole of the many many days and years of his life. He looked his last at the rock shining relentless; he closed his eyes. . . . I think it was at this moment that Felicia was screaming for assistance. If only she had kept her place a moment longer she would have seen help at hand.

Something struck his face. A voice, not far off,

said, very quietly, "Be careful. Can you get at the rope? We will pull you up. One! two! three!" Hope gave him renewed strength, and with a clutch he raised his left hand and caught the saving rope. For three seconds he was drawn upwards, scraping the rock as he went: happily its hard smoothness now was in his favour. Bleeding, fainting, he found himself drawn up to a ledge overhead. His senses failed.

When he came to himself, Baxter was pouring brandy down his throat, and the Swiss guide was loosening his clothes. They had seen him in the distance. The guide had suddenly stopped short, and exclaimed,

"Good heavens! that man must be mad. Where is he going to?" and pointed out Jasper's peril to the Colonel.

"We must go back," said the Colonel, hastily. . . . .

"I think I owe you my life," said Jasper, hoarsely, but quite naturally, looking up with bloodshot eyes at Aurelius.

"Nonsense!" said the Colonel, kindly, "it was Melchior here who spied you on your perch."

CHAPTER XII.

DA CAPO.

WHILE the travellers delay, the rocks are lighting up to bronze, to gold, to purple. The Wetterhorn is burning crimson-limned; the Mettelberg rocks are turning to splendid hue, the Vieschhorns answer like flaming beacons, and the great Eiger is on fire. But the hills to the east are shadowy mist upon palest ether, and a faint cloud like a sigh drifts along their ridge. So night comes on with solemn steps. Now the Wetterhorn is dying, the Vieschhorn pales to chillest white, though its summits are still flashing, rose-colour, flame-like, delicate. The people look up on their way, figures in the valley stand gazing at the wondrous peace overhead, they gaze and drink their fill of the evening, and then the lingering benediction is gone with a breath. The rocks are cold and dead, the ether is changed from incandescence to veiled dimness. Nothing seems left but the sound of the stream, which before was hardly heard, but which now takes up the tale, rushing through the ravine fresh and incessant. A star appears, the washerwoman's window lights up in the valley.

"Will you tea in the balcony?" the waiter asks, coming up with a lamp, which he sets on the little table by Flora's elbow.

"Nong," says the lady, "dedang;" and she looks at her watch and wonders why they are all so late. Then again she reflects with some satisfaction that Mr. Bracy and the two girls are not likely to get into much mischief alone, and *that* Colonel is safe out of the way. Mrs. Bracy begins to grow hungry and impatient for her family's return. They are quite absorbed in their own arrangements; they forget everything else. As usual, the spirit suffered from the matter's delay, and the temper also being frail and troublesome, seemed to trouble our poetess. When Pringle, Felicia's maid, came into the salle, to ask, a little anxiously, at what hour Mrs. Bracy was expecting them home, Flora snubbed Pringle as that personage was not accustomed to be snubbed, and sent her off in high dudgeon. A minute after, the woman returned, quite changed, with a curious scared face.

"Oh, ma'am!" she said, "come out here; there's a boy from the shalley. He says—he says—I can't understand. The cook is talking to him. Oh, ma'am!"

Flora jumped up, with more activity than she usually showed, and hurried out into the passage, where, surely enough, a crowd stood round a boy, dressed in common peasant's clothes, who was emphatically describing something—a fall—a scream. Poor Mrs. Bracy turned very cold, and forgot to analyse her emotions as she pushed her way through the guides and waiters.

"What, what?" she said. "Speak English, can't you? What does he say?"

"Your gentlemen 'ave met with accident," said one of the waiters. "De young lady she see him—call for guide to help; dis young man come down to tell you."

Then the young man said something in an undertone.

Poor Mrs. Bracy, almost beside herself now, asked with a sort of scream, "Who was hurt? Was it her husband? was it Jasper?"

The boy didn't know, the waiter explained. "He could tell nothing, only that it was a gentleman who had fallen a long way from the Kulm Hotel. Would Madame please give a trinkgeld; he had run all the way with the news?"

For the next two hours the poor old poetess, brought back to everyday anxiety and natural feeling, suffered a purgatory sufficient to wipe out many and many an hour of selfish ease and hallucination. She ordered guides, brandy, *chaise-à-porteurs*, for herself and Pringle. No porters were to be had at that hour, not at least in sufficient numbers to carry so heavy a lady over the dark and uneven roads. Horses then. Two tired steeds were at length led up to the door, upon one of which the poor lady was hoisted, Pringle devotedly following. So they set forth heroically, with two guides apiece, with brandy, with lanterns, and blankets, which Mrs. Bracy insisted on taking.

I cannot find it in my heart to describe that long, black, jolting terrifying progress, the bumps and slips, the horrors, the brawling streams, the crumbling mountain ways along which they climbed.

"Fear nothing," said the guides; but, as they spoke, Pringle's horse came down on its knees, and Pringle gave a wild shriek. So they toiled on, over resounding bridges, up slippery paths, under dark thickets, coming out into a great open alp. Suddenly two huge black forms seemed to rise up, and bear slowly down upon them.

The guides only laughed rudely. "Kühe, Kühe," said they, and then by degrees horns loomed out, and a heavy snuffling breath came through the darkness. The poor women were somewhat reassured. I do not know whether they ever would have

reached the top of the long weary pass, which
mounted in a long rocky ladder before them. Mrs.
Bracy's horse had in its turn come down, and was
scarcely roused by many an oath, as it stood trembling beneath its quavering burden. One lantern
had gone out, and could not be lighted again.
Pringle was crying—when suddenly there was a
pause—one of the porters said "Hist!" The second
ceased swearing at the horse, to listen.

"What is it?" says Mrs. Bracy. "Quoi?"

"People coming this way," said the man.

"I hear 'em talking, mem," says Pringle, hysterically.

Every moment the sound came clearer and
nearer. At a turn of the path a light appeared
overhead, then another and another; the tramp of
feet, the sound of men talking, and then could it
be?—a laugh coming out of the darkness—a real
hearty laugh.

Poor old Flora threw up her arms as she recognised her husband's voice, and burst into hearty,
unaffected tears of relief, excitement, and fatigue.
All must be well, or Mr. Bracy would not have burst
out laughing in the dark, at such an hour, on such
a road.

A minute more, it was a scene of greeting, exclamations, embraces, a snorting of horses, a waving

of lanterns. Mr. Bracy was ahead, running downhill, supported on either side by a porter. He was much overcome, and filled with admiration by his wife's devotion. There was something peculiar in his manner.

"Noble woman!" said he. "What exertion! You should have some champagne, Flora, my love," he said; "it will revive you—quite revived by it myself. Have you brought any with you? Baxter, do you happen to have another bottle?"

Baxter! Poor Mrs. Bracy turned in horror and bewilderment, and by the lantern's light descried only too plainly Baxter and Felicia, arm-in-arm, coming down the steep path together, preceded by a guide with a lantern.

Shall I attempt to describe the descriptions, or to explain the explanations. Some seemed to be of so extraordinary a character, that Flora Bracy had to exercise all her self-command to listen to them in silence. But Jasper's safety had softened the poetic heart, and she was unaffectedly grateful to the Colonel for the rescue. Of course, as Baxter said, anyone would have done as much, but not the less there do happily exist certain unreasonable emotions of gratitude in human nature which influence it out of the balance of exact debtor and creditor account.

"Fact was, my dear," said Mr. Bracy, looking

round and dropping his voice, "the poor dear girl
had been so anxious and worked up on Jasper's
account, that when they all came suddenly on to
the platform, just as we had almost given them up,
she and Georgina both shrieked, and Felicia, I believe, rushed fainting into somebody's arms. The
Colonel's, I believe. It was all a confusion. I was
myself rather overcome. I was certainly concerned
when Jasper afterwards told me the guides had been
talking about Felicia and Baxter. If you had been
there it would have been most desirable: however,
Felicia soon recovered; we gave her champagne—
that champagne was really excellent, considering the
circumstances. Curious thing, Flora, my love, the
corks come out at a touch up in those high places.
It might interest you to see——"

"Do, Edgar, keep to the important subject in
question," said Flora, piteously, she was too completely crushed to be severe.

"You mean about—hum—hum—" says Mr. Bracy,
getting rather breathless. "Jasper first gave me a
hint, and then the fact is, Baxter himself came up
in the most gentlemanly manner, and told us both
it was an old affair, that until now he had never had
any certainty of his affection being returned."

"And you, Edgar, placed in this most responsible
situation, what did you say?" asked his wife.

"I said, 'Colonel, I'll only ask you one question, which of the girls is it?' for I heard them both scream;" here Mr. Bracy stopped. A detachment from the rear joined them, Miss Bracy walking (she was too nervous to ride), and Jasper himself comfortably jogging down upon Georgina's mule.

The lovers meanwhile straggled off with their guide by some short by-road. They seemed to have wings, some sudden power that made them forget fatigue, darkness, length of way, that bore them safe over stones and briars, from step to step along the steep and slippery road; little Felicia felt no weariness, no loneliness: she had reached home at last. They reached the little bridge some ten minutes before the rest of the company, and there they stopped for a moment; while Melchior walked on to announce the safe return of the whole party. It was a wonderful minute, silent and shadowy, and fragrant with stars streaming in the dark sky overhead; the water was rushing into the night; as it flowed it seemed to flash with the dazzling lights of heaven, and to carry the stars upon its stream. The night breeze came across the plain and fanned their faces; they were alone, and a blessing of silent and unspeakable gratitude was theirs. And so, after all this long doubt, Aurelius and Felicia had come to the best certainty that exists in this perplexing world, the

S*

sacred conviction of love — that belongs to all estates and conditions of men, not only to the married, not only to the unmarried, but to all those who have grateful hearts.

END OF "DA CAPO."

F I N A.

SOME PASSAGES FROM AN OLD DIARY OF MISS WILLIAMSON'S.

THE child has a sweet inquisitive little face, and a pathetic voice. She looks hard at me when we meet on the stairs. Last Sunday I heard a crackling at my door, and, looking round, I saw my small fellow-lodger peeping in. "Come in," said I, making the first advances. "How do you do?" The little girl advanced shyly, looking about. I saw her looking at the china-pot full of roses, at me, at my pictures. But she did not appear quite satisfied. "Why do you live so high up?" she said. "You can't walk out in the garden as mamma does."

Fina—so they call her—lives on the ground floor, with her father and mother. The drawing-room floor is let to a fashionable barrister, who is out all day, and who only comes home to dress in splendour and white ties, and to drive off again in hansom cabs. *I* am only the second floor, and yet this seemed a very paradise of lodgings when I accidentally stumbled upon it one day on my way to Old Palace-square. A paradise with neither moth nor rust to corrupt, nor grasping landlady to peep through and steal. I think it was the sight of little Fina's face at the parlour window which attracted me. The housekeeper looked friendly, the house was clean and old-fashioned. I thankfully climbed my two flights, unpacked my possessions, and settled down. Elsewhere I am a governess, and go my rounds; but here everyday as I come back a transformation takes place. I hang up my waterproof, drop my claws and my instructive manner, tuck away my horns under my cap, and become a quiet, respectable, independent old lady, with cherry jam and seed-cake in my cupboard, an evening paper, and a comfortable arm-chair; but all these advantages do not seem to impress little Fina.

"Shouldn't you like to walk in the garden," persists the child; "come here, Fina, and look out of my window," I reply; "you see I have my garden up here."

This little street of ours runs from the main road into Old Palace-square, and my sitting-room windows open to the street, but my bed-room overlooks the gardens of the square, the many green lawns and flower-beds. This little corner is almost like the country. A thrush sings in the chestnut-tree beyond the wall, and awakens with the dawn; little Fina stands on the wooden bench at the end of our narrow inclosure and wistfully peeps over the bricks, at the children at play in the big garden next to ours. These big gardens act the part of benevolent protectors to us, their humbler neighbours. They send us whiffs of apple-blossom and lilac, notes of birds, and stray sprigs of green.

The garden of the house to which I go every day is the one next to ours. It is the corner house of Old Palace-square, and has been let for the season to an old lady and her son and her grandchildren. There is an air of prosperity about its well-cleaned windows and brightly-scrubbed brasswork, and its respectable, over-fed butler. Mrs. Ellis, in her Indian shawls, is all in keeping with the place; she is a friend of my old friend Lady Z., who recommended me to apply for the situation. I had been afraid my inability to teach music might have stood in my way, but in this case music was not wanted. The Colonel did not wish his daughters to learn music, I was told. It seemed to me a curious fancy. I was a little late this morning; and, as I was hurrying down stairs, on my way to my pupils, I met my little girl again. I am fond of most children, but this one interests me specially. The parlour door was open as I passed, and Fina's father was coming out. The child darted away from my side to meet him, and began dancing and swinging by his hand. "Take care, little Fina; take care, you imp!" he cried; "you will make me drop my violin." He was carrying a violin-case under one arm. He was a big man, burly, and near six foot high, with an honest, somewhat careworn face, and a grizzled, shock head of hair. I believe he is the Francis Arnheim whose name I have seen in big letters outside the Albert Hall and elsewhere. Big as he is, his little girl seems at her ease with him. She paid no attention to her father's remonstrances, and went on with her wild gymnastics. "Mamma, come and take this little demon!" cried Arnheim; and then the mother came, smiling, to the rescue, and put her arms round the child and carried her off. I could not help thinking of this little scene five minutes later, as I stood on the doorstep of my employer's house in Old Palace-square.

The Colonel himself was going out for a ride, and impatiently waiting to be off. The poor children had come up with a shout from the garden of the square. Edgar, the boy, a handsome little fellow about eight years old, rushed across the road and, in his excitement, tumbled over the Colonel's shiny boots. "Here comes Grasshopper, here she comes —Papa, do, do let me have one ride," says little Edgar.

"I can't have this noise in the street," says the Colonel. "You should have been at your lessons

long before this." With this rebuke, which applied
to the dilatory governess as well as to the pupils,
the Colonel sprang upon his horse, never looking
back, and caracoled erectly down the square to the
admiration of the young ladies' school opposite, the
baker's boy at the area gate, and the old mother at
the drawing-room window. His friendly little audience
of children meanwhile retreated somewhat disconcerted to the schoolroom.

There was not much in all this—not much, only
everything. The musician's voice had seemed to
me that of a father, but this was no father's voice.
The little shabby lodging where Fina dwelt seemed
to me a real home, the big house, with its stair-
rods and buckram and well-trained servants, a sort
of lodging-house only. The old grandmother half
asleep in her Indian shawls—a soft old lady like an
owl—was the one bit of home to me in the big
house. She was, what she looked, a lady of the
old easy-going school—well bred, well born. At
times she seemed rather afraid of her son and her
eldest daughter. There was a second daughter I
had not yet seen, who was coming home, the children told me.

"Aunt Josephine is *such* a dear," said little
Edgar, confidentially; "isn't she, Josie? *She* will let

us come to tea with you. Don't ask Aunt Bessie, *she* always says no."

I could quite imagine this. Miss Ellis was a second edition of the Colonel—high heels, tight straps, stiff linen, sharp voice included.

Aunt Josephine, the younger sister, took after her mother. The very first morning she was at home she looked into the school-room with a friendly face to see what we were all about. She was hospitably welcomed by the young people. Mary, the eldest girl, pushed up a chair, Edgar gave it a thump to make it comfortable, little Josie thrust a lesson-book into her aunt's hand. "You stop and do lessons, too," said she.

"Very well," said Aunt Josephine. And after this she got into the way of coming every day.

One morning she was reading by the window while we were at work when we heard the Colonel's voice outside calling hastily for Miss Ellis; then the door opened and he looked in: he was red, odd, excited. "Bessie is out; I want you, Josephine," he said. He appeared to be in great perturbation: he left the door open, and we heard his heels on the oil-cloth in the hall as he walked up and down, talking emphatically.

"He is here; I saw him myself. We shall have him here." Then a sort of burst from Aunt Josephine—"Oh! perhaps she is with him. I *must* tell mamma—indeed I must."

The three children had all left off their sums and were listening with the deepest attention. "You had better shut the door, Edgar," said I; and Edgar obeyed very slowly.

"It's about Aunt Mary," said little Josie, nodding her head. "Aunt Josephine always cries when it is about Aunt Mary."

"Hush, Josie!" said little Mary; and as she spoke we heard a sob from Aunt Josie in the hall. It was a curious little family scene, but it did not concern me. I forbade all talking, and did my best to keep my little pupils quiet and attentive to their lessons. They were good, lovable children, and flourished upon somewhat arid soil, as one has seen little flowers upspringing in rocky, unlikely places. Although I forbade discussion, I found myself puzzling over it all that evening as I sat alone with my lamp, and wondering why Aunt Mary was not to be mentioned. Had she disgraced herself? What crime had she committed? Then came a something to distract me from these fruitless digressions, and to carry me far, far away from my lonely corner—a lovely voice, Mendelssohn's voice, calling, singing of many a familiar home strain to me. Fina's father was playing down below on his violin, and somehow, irresistibly drawn and attracted, I presently found myself standing at the foot of the stairs in the moonlight, listening, absorbed, to his music. There also stood the landlady, raised from her kitchen. "Aint it beautiful, mem?" said she. We were both rather foolishly disconcerted when the back parlour door suddenly opened upon us. The room was full of harmony and light; the floor seemed scattered over with music-books. Someone was standing by a music-stand playing the violin. Many candles were burning. Out of all this radiance little Fina came darting, and calling out, "Mamma, here is my lady!" And then the mother, with a very sweet, gentle face and manner, came out and invited me in.

After this it became a usual thing for me to go down when Mr. Arnheim was at home. As soon as his practice began little Fina used to come running up to my room to summon me. I am not sure that the music was the best thing to be found in that shabby back parlour; the peace, the moderation, the mutual trust and confidence of that little family touched me as much as the wonderful strains of Arnheim's violin. His playing was unequal, but there was a certain quality about it which I can scarcely describe—a suggestion beyond the music. I used to think Mrs. Arnheim had caught that some-

thing in her face—in her lovable eyes. I could not
think who it was she reminded me of at times.
Meanwhile I sit peacefully listening and watching
her as she turns over her husband's leaves. The
back windows are open to the garden, where little
Fina is hopping about in the dusk. Mendelssohn
speaks, and we are all silent and spell-bound.

May 1.

My friend Lady Z. has written to offer me her
carriage for to-morrow, and I think it will add to
the interest of my long-promised party if we drive
down first to Roehampton, as she suggests, lunch in
her garden, and fill our baskets with rhododendrons.
Kind Aunt Josephine has asked leave for the children to come; and my friend Fina and her mother
are to join the little expedition. Last night, as I
was going up to my room, I met Fina blushing and
with entreating looks. The landlady's little boy was
at home for the holidays. He was such a good little
boy, and helped his mother with the knives and
boots. Might he come for the drive on the box?

Fina's eyes danced with delight when I agreed
to this arrangement. My preparations of cold chicken
and salad are all made, and nicely packed by the
landlady, whose little son Dan is also, I do believe,

to be parboiled for the occasion, brushed, and scrubbed, and trussed.

Is there anything so sweet, so hopeful as an early spring morning without cold wind or spite in the air only a gentle awakening to sunshine and cheerful sounds? The birds have been singing since the dawn; the trees and green plants have come out with a new flood of colour; London puts on its loveliest spring veils and lights, and tosses its blue sky with floating clouds; the parks are a burst of perfume and May essence; the shrubs glow with white and crimson; the very streets are abloom! Just now, when I looked out from my window, I saw two ragged figures dragging a flower-cart—a creaking load of gold and dazzling colour—at which everyone turned to look. These were only itinerant flower-dealers; but Titania herself could not have conjured up a more lovely rainbow. The passers-by stopped to look; the little girl from below ran out and changed her coppers for lovely new lamps of white narcissus—of pale blue hyacinth. I saw a bunch in Mrs. Arnheim's waistband when she came out all ready for our start. She also was dressed in muslin, with a pretty straw hat tied under her chin, and a look of youth and enjoyment in her gentle grey eyes which I had

scarcely ever seen before. She sprang into the carriage almost as eagerly as little Fina herself. The
coachman pulled my hamper up beside him on the
box; Dan followed the hamper; the horses, with a
great deal of clattering and jumping, set off, the sun
made merry all along the way as we drove by the
pleasant old roads that lead from London to the
river and beyond it. I specially remember two red
cows eating dazzling green grass under a staring
pink apple-tree. "Look at the flower-tree," said little
Josie, pointing. She was the youngest of the party,
and chattered unceasingly for us all.

"What a funny name Fina is," said she. "Have
you a real name too?"

"My name is Josephine," said Fina; "but papa
always calls me Fina."

"Why, *my* name is Josephine," said Josie, "and
so is grandmamma's." And all the children exclaimed.

As the children talked, I looked up and caught
a strange, eager, half-hopeful, half-frightened expression in Mrs. Arnheim's face; and all of a sudden I
knew who it was she reminded me of at times—who
but my sleepy old lady in Old Palace-square?

"What is your name, Mrs. Arnheim?" I asked,
with some odd certainty of what her answer would be.

"Mary," she said, simply; and as she spoke her eyes filled with tears.

After luncheon the children played away to their hearts' content in lady Z.'s pretty old park. Mrs. Arnheim and I kept to the beaten paths and zinc benches; the children held a happy little woodland court in the shade of the trees, with music of birds overhead and childish laughter, with many orders and decorations of daisy and of primrose. Josie was enthroned on the branch of an old tree, the others gathered round. Little Dan was allowed to join the sports and meanwhile Mrs. Arnheim was asking me question after question — who was the little girl called Josephine, who was her grandmother; and as I answered she tried to speak—she faltered, then burst into tears, "Don't you guess it all, she sobbed. Yes, she is my mother, my own mother, and I did not even know we were at her very door. Oh! Miss Williamson, she *must* relent, she must take me to her heart once more. If it were not for my brother she would have done so long, long ago. When I go there they will not admit me. When I write they send me back my letters. This time, when we came to England I could make no more advances. I had been too bitterly wounded."

It is difficult to understand how some people can have the courage to be unforgiving, day after day,

week after week. They go to sleep, they wake up
again; they hear the birds sing; they see the sun
shine upon the just and the unjust; a thousand
blessings are theirs; but still they hold out and refuse their own blessing to the offenders. They hear
of sorrows that can never be healed; they hear of
joys befalling their fellow-men; they realise life and
death, and it does not occur to them that there is
no death like that of coldness and estrangement.
Against the inevitable, warm hearts can hold their
own; but the avoidable, the self-inflicted pangs of
life, what is there to be said for them? This kind
old lady, Mrs. Ellis by name, who was good to the
poor, thoughtful for her dependants, affectionate to
her friends, showed a stern and unforgiving spirit
towards one person which seemed utterly at variance
with her whole life and nature. This one person
was the daughter she had loved best of all her
children, who had left her home one day and married without her mother's consent. Arnheim had
been Mary's music master. The family could not
forget it.

All the way home I sat turning over one scheme
and another in my mind for bringing the mother
and daughter together without any chance of interference from the Colonel or Miss Ellis. Miss Josephine I knew would help me, but she was young

9*

and timid, and it seemed to me safest to act on my own responsibility.

Mrs. Arnheim had lent me her parlour for tea. It was pleasanter than mine, and opened on the garden; and as we were all eating our bread-and-butter and strawberries Arnheim looked in. I saw him give a quick, anxious look at his wife, who sat silent and with a drooping head.

"Here is papa," cries Fina; "now he will play to us. Papa, they do want to hear some music. Please, play, and we will dance mulberry-bush in the garden, and Dan shall come too."

"I want Dan to go for a message for me first," said I, a vision of the Colonel's wrath rising before my eyes if Dan were allowed to dance in the ring with the other children.

"Dear Mrs. Ellis," I wrote, "would you be so very good and kind as to come in for five minutes, and see my happy little party. Yours sincerely,
                              MARY WILLIAMSON."

After a time the children became riotous over their mulberry-bush game, and Arnheim began to play another measure, and then by degrees they quieted down and came to the window to listen. Dan and Edgar exchanged a few cuffs in the twilight; the little girls listened; and I sat wondering what was to come of my note.

Presently there was a ring at the door, and I thought I could recognise the soft, lagging step of the old lady from the square.

"See who it is," I whispered to Mrs. Arnheim, who looked surprised, but got up quietly and went to the door. I followed her. The passage was dark, but the garden door was open, and the old lady had passed on to the garden door.

Then I heard a little cry from one or from the other—I know not which it was; their two voices sounded so alike.

"Oh, Mother!" said Mrs. Arnheim, springing forward, with both hands wildly put out.

"Mary! You! My child!" said the aged woman, surprised and overcome; and the two women were locked together in a long, close embrace. And then the two hearts so cruelly parted were beating together once more. . .

Neither the Colonel nor Miss Ellis could keep them asunder now. Tighter and closer the mother clasped her daughter; those fast enclosing arms clung to the truth, to the reality of life, to the love of past years. Mrs. Ellis was near the end of her long journey. Was she to let her child go now that she had found her again?

Arnheim, meanwhile, went on playing, quite unconscious of the scene just outside the door.   He
quietly travelled to the end of his melody.   His
beautiful music seemed singing in measure to that
best and holiest strain of peace and reconciliation.

END OF "FINA."

ACROSS THE PEAT-FIELDS.

CHAPTER I.

OLD MSS.

NOT long ago the children opened a drawer in my writing-table and found a little roll of dusty manuscript which I myself had written many years ago. It was a story in which some true things were told with others that were not true, all blended together in that same curious way in which, when we are asleep, we dream out allegories, and remembrances, and indications that we scarcely recognise when we are awake. Story-telling is, in truth, a sort of dreaming, from which the writer only quite awakes when the last proof is corrected. These visions seem to haunt one, and to contend with realities, and at times to flash into definite shape, and voice, and motion, and to hold their own almost independently of our will, and to impress us, as real voices and impulses do in everyday existence.

When the children, who take a faithful interest in my performances, brought me this dusty packet

I read it through, and once more found myself in a little village in France, which I had scarcely thought of for years and years. There it stood among its plains, sunning itself in the autumn rays; all the people who used to live there with us came marching out of the drawer, bringing fruit in their hands, rolling barrows piled with golden pumpkins, carrying great baskets of purple plums, or sweet greengages oozing golden juice, great jugs of milk, and wheaten loaves baked in the country ovens. Not only people, but the bygone animals came too out of this ark. A black retriever making for the water, the turkey-cocks perching on our doorsteps, the little black hen with the crooked bill; the poor tortoiseshell cat, who died of hunger, shut up in the cellar below the kitchen. We had a cook—a hateful woman—who had once tried to poison the poor creature, and who laughed at our dismay when we learnt its ultimate fate. No one else had heard its cries. The rambling old place seemed made for some such tragedy, piled together with dark corners, hidden passages, stone flights, and heavy masonry. The walls were of thickest stone. There was a sort of dungeon under the flight of steps that led to the house-door, and the dining-room had two hiding-places opening on either side of the jam cupboard. All round the drawing-room a secret passage ran between the wall and the wooden panelling. This passage was lighted by a narrow window, all hidden by leaves of the vine-tree. The drawing-room windows opened into a sweet garden full of flowers and straggling greenery. At the end of the walk by the vine wall stood a little pavilion, with a pointed roof and a twirling weathercock, with casements north, east, and west. This little pavilion seemed to guard the entrance of the village. People said that the old farm had once been a hunting-lodge built by Henry IV., who came here with his Court. I could imagine any one of the old pictures I had seen in the Louvre and elsewhere made alive, the gay cavalcade sounding and galloping away, disappearing along the highway; horses prancing, squires following, horns sounding, and scarfs flying in the air. Sometimes the King ruled at the Château de Visy, so the legend ran; but the château was the Queen's and the hunting-lodge was the King's, and the little pavilion where we girls all did our lessons together, and blotted our German exercises, had been built for some aigretted lady of the Court.

Visy le Roi is a village not far from Corbeil, a well-known country town in France. It is a district where the sun sets across miles of flat spreading fields that are crossed and recrossed in every direction by narrow canals, of which the sluggish waters reflect the willows planted along their course. These streams are darkened by the colour of the banks on either side. The earth is nearly black; the water is stained by strange tints. The country is sombre with peat-fields, and here and there are peat-manu-factories, standing lonely against the sky. When the light blazes it is reflected on the waters as they flow with a certain sluggish persistent tide. Every here and there at crossways are deep pools where lilies and green tangles are floating on the brown eddies. Sometimes of an evening, when the sun sets over the black fields, long-drawn chords of light strike against the stems of the poplar-trees, and then their quaint mop heads seem on fire, while the flames roll down from the West with vapour and with murky splendour. The figures passing along the roads on the way homewards, the blue blouses, the country-women carrying their baskets on their arms or their faggots on their backs, are strangely illumined by these last beams of daylight. Some of Millet's sketches at Paris a year ago brought a remembrance to my mind of the roads and country places that I had haunted in my early youth. Few painters have drawn such wide fields as he; plains stretching so far—hours so long, as I remember them in those days, when they passed with strangely slow and heavy footsteps. The hours are shorter now. The plains are sooner crossed; horizons close in. Hope is less, and less deferred.

The inhabitants of Visy le Roi might be bakers or grocers in public; in private, after business hours, and at the backs of their houses, they were comfortable people, with pleasant gardens—in which they spent much of their time, among an abundance of pumpkins, of vine wreaths, of reflecting glass globes on wooden stems, and blue lupins. Some of the people in the village, finding the gardens at the back of their houses insufficient for their requirements, cultivated quadrangles outside the village, where they would water their rose-trees quietly of summer evenings.

The Maire of Visy le Roi was very proud of his garden, which was neatly spread out in front of his stone house, and ornamented by two large black balls reflecting each other and the street, and our opposite gateway, and our dining-room windows, and his tidy plots of marigolds and scarlet-runners, which were our admiration. He used to be specially active on summer evenings, and might be seen clipping, and chopping, and brushing away insects. He was not married in those days; he settled in Normandy after his first marriage, and sold his property at Visy. In fact, circumstances had made the place distasteful to him. He was a sensitive, kind-hearted man, although a somewhat absurd one. One of our party, a young French lady, who has since made a name for herself, was a good musician, and evening after evening I have sat listening to the flow of her music and the scrapings of M. Fontaine's violin. I made bold to put them into a book long after, but here they are in the catgut. How plainly these strains still sound coming out of the darkened room, with the figures sitting round; the windows are open to the dim garden, and I can still hear the dinning accompaniment of the grasshoppers outside whistling their evening song to the rising stars.

My granduncle, who was of an ingenious turn of mind, had come to Visy to try a machine he had invented, and to make experiments in the manufacture of peat-fuel. It is certain that with his machine, and the help of an old woman and a boy, he could produce as many little square blocks of firing in a day as M. Mérard, the rival manufacturer, in three, with all his staff, including his cook and his carter's son. The carter himself, a surly fellow, had refused to assist in the factory. It is true that our machine cost about 300l. to start with, and that it was constantly getting out of order and requiring the doctoring of a Paris engineer; but, setting that aside, as Monsieur Fontaine proved to us after an elaborate calculation, it was clear that a saving of 35 per cent. was effected by our process.

The engineer from Paris having failed us on two occasions, I believe that my granduncle had at one time serious thoughts of constructing a mechanical engineer, who was to keep the whole thing in order, and only to require an occasional poke himself to continue going. I remember once seeing a wooden foot wrapped up in cotton wool in a box in our workshop, but I believe this being went no further. The old woman's wages, with the boy's, were fifteen francs a week, amounting to about seven pounds for the three months we were at Visy. The Franken-stein's foot alone cost twelve pounds, so that it is easy to reckon how other more complicated organs would have run up the bill. I asked my uncle once whether the creature when complete would be content to live in the shed, or insist on coming home of an evening and joining the family circle. "Who can tell?" said my granduncle, laughing; "perhaps it may turn out an agreeable member of society, and Fontaine himself will be cut out in his attentions to Mademoiselle Mérard."

Old Mérard was the rival manufacturer. He came down in his slippers one day to inspect our designs; he did not think much of them, and declined to purchase the patent. He and Madame

Mérard, and Mademoiselle Léonie, were, so he told us, starting for their estate in Normandy. Madame Mérard and her daughter never missed the bathing season, and preferred being accompanied by him; he was a tidy-looking old fellow, Madame was a dark and forbidding-looking person—a brunette, my polite old uncle called her, when I complained that she frightened me with her moustache and gleaming white teeth. Madame Mérard had a strange effect upon people's nerves. I always felt as if she was going to bite me. As for Mademoiselle Léonie, she was a washed-out, vapid, plaintive personage, in grey alpaca and plaid ribbons. She embroidered, she sang out of tune, she shuddered at the mention of a Protestant. She would have been a nonentity but for her ill temper, which fascinated Fontaine. I never could otherwise account for the attraction which our friend seemed to find in her society.

CHAPTER II.

BLACK CANALS AND YELLOW PUMPKINS.

AFTER the Mérards' departure for Petit-port, we saw a great deal of M. le Maire. He was a sociable creature, and consoled himself for his Léonie's absence by various gentle flirtations in the village. Our life would have been monotonous but for his cheerful visits and friendly introductions. All our acquaintance in the place we owed to him. He introduced us to the new-made Lords of the Manor, the Fourniers at the Castle (he brought us a message from Madame Fournier requesting us to call there any day our religion might permit), the Mérards, the fascinating Madame Valmy, Captain Thompson, our compatriot; upon all these persons we called at Fontaine's suggestion, and escorted by him. But we did not greatly care for society. Some of us were too old, some of us were too young, to need much company beside our own. We young ones lived in good society. Poets sang to us in the mornings under the shady vine trellis, and of evenings by lamplight and by moonlight; we had the company of philosophers too, and of romancers, charming in those days with an art which I can remember with a sort of wonder. So we rose betimes, worked and rested, studying in barns and trellised bowers, exploring the farms and farmyards round about. When we had written our exercises, practised our fingers upon the piano, closed our lesson-books, agricultural arts awaited us. Muslin bags had to be made for the sweet heavy bunches of ripening grapes. The pumpkins had to be met, counted, disposed of. I remember one dewy morning when the first pumpkin opened fire, if I may so describe its advent. Next day there were twenty large golden disks, and then from every side they upheaved, growing upon us hour by hour, multiplying, rolling in, in irresistible numbers; hanging from the tops of the walls. From every corner these monstrous creatures encircled us. Poor Fontaine was in despair; it was a plague of pumpkins. "There are those who like pumpkin soup," said he, doubtfully. Here we all cried out, protesting we had had pumpkin soup every day for a week; we did not like it all. But my cousin, Mary Williamson, the housekeeper, declared that it was absolutely necessary, and so the remainder of our stay was embittered to us by the tides of this milky, seedy, curd-like mixture.

Our visit to the Fourniers was a very solemn

event. From the very first Monsieur Fontaine had been anxious that we should realise the glories of the Castle.

"You will see—pure Henri Quatre—Monsieur Fournier bought it direct from the Mesnils, and has not yet refurnished the reception-rooms. The Mesnils had owned it for years, but the late Count ruined the family, and they were forced to sell at his death. Madame la Comtesse signed the papers before me as well as her son. She was in a fury, poor woman! I tried to soothe her; she flung the pen into my face; her son, Monsieur Maurice, apologised. 'My dear friend,' I said to him, 'do not mention it.'"

Monsieur Fontaine came to fetch us on the appointed day. My cousins could not join us, but my uncle put on his short round cloak, and we set off together. On the way along the village street, Monsieur Fontaine gave us information about the various inhabitants. "Ah! there goes the doctor; that good Poujac; he is the most amiable character. Monsieur le Curé says he never had a more devout parishioner, and yet if I were seriously ill, I should send to Corbeil, I think, for further advice. Madame Valmy has the greatest confidence in him. He nursed her husband in his last illness. It was most alarming for her—it was cholera. Poor Valmy died within twenty-four hours; she is only now out of mourning.

She has passed the winter at Paris—I should like to pass the winter at Paris," sighed Fontaine, "but my duties keep me here, and when my vacation comes," he said consciously, "I am to remain a fortnight with my friends, the Mérards, at Petit-port, for the bathing season. Mademoiselle Léonie's health requires sea-bathing; she has not the physique of Mademoiselle Pauline at the Castle."

As he spoke, we had a vision of Mademoiselle Pauline herself in the distance, actively trudging alongside the canal. Monsieur Fontaine became very much excited as he pointed her out to us. She was followed by a maid-servant carrying a basket, and walking quietly, with long country footsteps, and wearing a white coiffe, a handkerchief across her shoulders, and a big apron with pockets. Her young mistress, unconscious of Fontaine's signals, sometimes hurried ahead, sometimes lagged behind to gather dock-leaves, branches of green, and marsh-mallows, of which she had made a sort of wreath, bound together by broad blades of grass. I could see the two heads passing between the willow stumps; some bird wheeled round overhead, and returned to its nest in a willow tree; some water-rat splashed from its hole at the root of an alder. The young person walking ahead hearing this splashing, stopped short and went down on her knees among the grasses; the maid-servant, who had long since out-grown the age of weasels and water-rats, and had matured to domestic interests, went on her way.

What a strange feeling it gives to write of all this that happened so long ago, vividly flashing be-fore one's mind like the splash of the water-rat. I remember how the willows stood at intervals with their black stumpy stems, how all the purples and golds of the evening were reflected in the peat-stained water, shining in the green foliage and on the bricks of the old walls of the park.

"Mademoiselle!" said the Maire, politely stepping forward.

Pauline, still upon her knees, looked round into our faces while the Maire introduced us, and the water-rat darted away. She scrambled up; her dress was all dabbled with water, smeared with black earth, and also on fire with the evening light; so was her hair, which was oddly dressed in two twisted horns in the fashion of those days. There was something rude and honest about Mademoiselle Pauline which attracted me to her. She had a thick waist, country shoes; she wore a blue ribbon with a medal round her neck. She had pudgy red hands. She acknowledged Fontaine's elaborate in-troduction by squaring her elbows, with an awkward bob of the head which she had copied from her father. Then she turned and said to my uncle in tolerable English, "My papa and mama are at the house; will you come to see them?" and then she led the way without another word. There was a low door in the wall at which Pauline stopped, pushing with her shoulder and giving a violent jerk.

"Allow me, mademoiselle. You will hurt yourself," exclaimed Fontaine, quite shocked.

"Take care, my dear young lady," said uncle Joseph; "a small wedge inserted into the opening—"

But Pauline had burst open the door, and there was no more to be said. We all walked into the park, which was darkly overgrown, as French parks are apt to be, but not without a certain dim charm of its own. Long vistas glimmered, and narrow avenues of trees ran in every direction. The great gates at the entrance of the chief avenue were half sunk into the earth; the ivies were clinging to the rusty hinges. The Court and its gay company had passed away, leaving it all to silence. For those who were to come after only a sign remained from the past generation to that which was to come—a stone with a herald's mark for us to note as we go by—some symbol of glories that are not quite over yet for impressionable people. And then we in turn hang up our trophies, names, and records, dumbly

appealing for goodwill and sympathy to those who
are to come after, and so we pass on our way. The
maid walked first, then came Pauline swinging her
arms, then followed my uncle and Fontaine of the
springing step. The park led to an open space in
front of the old house, and a terrace, upon which M.
and Madame Fournier were seated enjoying the
evening air. They had coffee-cups on the little green
table between them. M. Fournier was in his shirt-
sleeves, Madame Fournier's hair was neatly combed
and arranged with many pins. She did not wear a
cap, as do English matrons. She was like her
daughter in appearance; but, although prettier, she
had less expression. Neither she nor her husband
troubled themselves about Henry IV. and his hunt.
They put a large billiard table in the hall, set a
maid to darn stockings in a window, placed a green-
baize-covered piano exactly in the centre of the
drawing-room, saw that the floor was polished, so
that Pauline could slide from one end to the other
in her chaussons, and prepared to enjoy the fruits
of their many years' labour in peace. But there was
still something to be done. Pauline, notwithstanding
her short frocks, her scrambles, her tails of plaited
hair, was eighteen, and of an age to marry. "His
daughter's establishment occupies Fournier very
anxiously," the Maire had already explained; "se-

veral propositions have been made, but he has his own ideas. Mademoiselle Pauline herself as yet only thinks of running wild. Hers is a wonderful activity!"

"She inherits it from her papa," Madame Fournier used to say. She was fat and lazy herself, and took her exercise chiefly in nodding from her chair; she would gladly have seen her daughter more like other girls, and used to protest placidly from the chimney-corner, "Would you believe it, Monsieur Fontaine, my daughter drags the roller unassisted for an hour a day! It is inconceivable."

"Excellent gymnastics, mama," says papa Fournier, cheerfully. "Don't you interfere with my course of hygiene."

Next time I walked up to the Château. I was amused to meet Pauline actively occupied, as her mother had described, dragging a huge roller over the grass. The young lady stopped on seeing me coming, wiped her brow, and sent a gardener for a glass of beer, which she tossed off at a draught. Her manners were not attractive at first sight, but one got used to them by degrees, and very soon Pauline and I had struck up a girlish intimacy.

She was a kind and warm-hearted girl, gentle enough in reality, although she seemed so abrupt

and determined at first. She was dogmatic and
conceited; she had a habit of telling long and prosy
stories all about her own exploits and wonderful
penetration, but this was only want of habit of the
world. Her confidence in others made her a bore,
perhaps, but it made one love her too. She had
plenty of sympathy and intelligence. She had never
read any books, or known anybody outside the walls
of her home. It was a lonely life that she had lived,
with the garden-roller and her dogs for playfellows,
roaming within the gloomy gates of the park, or
among the black fields and creeping waters that
surrounded it. But she was happy enough; she was
free to come and go as she liked. The tranquil
commonplace of home was made dear to her by her
father's trusting love; even her mother's placid jealousy was part of it all.

"Before my brother died," she said one day,
"mama did not mind little things as she does now.
That was years ago—before I can remember. I am
the only child," she said, with a sigh, "and all their
fortune is for me, they say. They have bought this
big house for me; it is part of my *dot;* it was the
de Mesnils' once." Then she shrugged her broad
shoulders. "I shall be a great deal richer and in a
much better position than Claudie de Mesnil, and
yet I assure you Madame la Comtesse would scarcely

allow her daughter to speak to me. She thinks people who are not noble are scarcely human beings. I am a good bourgeoise, and I am not ashamed of it. I might like aristocrats better if they were more like Monsieur Maurice," said Pauline. "That day his mother was rude, and sent her daughter away from me when I spoke to her, he looked really sorry, and came up to mama to try and make up. I was nearly crying, but I would not let them see it. We had gone to offer that detestable woman the Château for the summer. She would not take it, so we left it shut up. Another year you might have it if you liked, and you must come and stay with me next week when your uncle goes back to Paris. You don't know me yet; but I know you, and I am sure we shall be good friends. Shake hands," and she held out her hand. It was very red and broad, but its grasp was cordial. "I will come and see you to-morrow after breakfast. Is it true that Protestants fast every day but Sunday? I should not like that," says Pauline, making a horrible face. "I did not like the English till I knew you." Here, I suppose, I flushed up.

"Good morning," I said, very stiffly. "I might say just the contrary. I *did* like the French until——"

"Nonsense. You like me very much," said Pauline. "I shall come and see you to-morrow, after our breakfast."

I took my way along the canal, and she walked off under the trees, whistling and swinging her arms.

———

CHAPTER III.

AN INVENTORY.

I AFTERWARDS discovered that Pauline did these
things a little out of bravado. She was not really
vulgar, though she did vulgar things, and would
swing her arms, rub her eyes, yawn in one's face in
the most provoking manner at times. I have heard
her exclaim, "Ah! bah!" just as the peasants did
down in the village. This was what she said when
her father told her one day that an uncle of M. de
Mesnil, an old bachelor living in Paris, had, upon
some general expression of Monsieur Fournier's
goodwill towards the young dispossessed proprietor
of the Château, asked him pointblank what he would
say in the event of Maurice de Mesnil coming forward as a suitor for the hand of Mademoiselle
Fournier.

"There! that is just like you," cried Madame
Fournier, strangely flustered for her. "You tell one
this when it is too late; you never consult me, never
say one word till the whole thing has blown over.
Pauline, I don't know whether you or your father is

the most childish and incapable. I have no doubt,
M. Fournier, you never gave any answer at all!"

"I gave an answer," said Fournier, gravely.

"Well!" said Madame Fournier, "what did you
say?"

Fournier shrugged his shoulders. "It was absurd," said he; "that was what I said. If they had
not been so unfortunate, I might have told them
that their suggestion seemed an impertinence."

"An impertinence, papa," said Pauline. "M.
Maurice never would be impertinent. He knew nothing about it. I could not have believed you to be
so prejudiced," and she suddenly leaped over a little
rail that happened to be in her way, and walked off.
Madame Fournier looked after her. When Fournier
spoke again, his wife answered him so sharply for
her, that I thought it more discreet to leave the
worthy couple to themselves. I could not find
Pauline anywhere in the park, but on my way back
to the house I met Fournier walking thoughtfully
along with his hands in his pockets.

"Have you not found Pauline?" he asked. "Has
she run off? Are you not great friends, you two?
My little Pauline," he went on, speaking to himself;
"she is a treasure. Whoever wins her will have
found a treasure. Her mother would have her
different—a fine lady; not so would I. She is true

and innocent and courageous, and tender to those who belong to her home. I am thankful to have so good a child." And so he walked on.

Presently someone came up from behind and caught me round the neck with a sudden pair of arms.

"You never saw me, you little blind creature," cries Pauline. "I have been peeping at you from behind the bushes. You looked so nice there! Come—papa shall take us in the punt; that is a good bourgeois way of getting about. I saw him just now waiting down by the waterside." And there surely enough stood Monsieur Fournier, looking abstractedly across the canal at the willow stumps opposite.

It was in the punt, as we were sliding along the waters, with the lovely autumn gold lighting the dark banks, with the green leaves floating on the water and insects droning sleepily, and a sweet fragrance in the air, and a faint aroma of distant peat-fields, that M. Fournier said to his daughter, "Tell me, Pauline, is your mother right? Would you like me to think seriously of young de Mesnil for your husband?"

"I like him very much, papa," said Pauline, very composedly. "I would not wish to influence you or my mother, as I am sure you can judge far better

than I can. But if you ask me my wishes, I should
certainly be glad that you should consider M. de
Mesnil's proposition."

I opened my eyes in amazement. Was this—
was this the way in which a maiden yielded her
heart? Were they serious? They were quite serious,
and went on discussing the subject until the boat
ran aground. Then we had to clamber up the
banks and run home in the twilight, under the trees.

When Pauline asked me to spend a fortnight
with her after my uncle's return to Paris, I had
gladly consented, for I was sincerely interested by
my new friend. From some hints of Monsieur Fontaine's, I had imagined that under the circumstances
my presence might be thought out of place, but they
assured me that I was welcome, and Madame
Fournier kindly insisted.

"We are glad, miss," she said, "that our Pauline
should be cheered and distracted by the presence of
one of her own age. You young people understand
one another." When it was thus decided that I
should stay on with Pauline Fournier, the respite
was very welcome to me. We had all been very
happy in the little village, and not one of us but
felt sorry that the time was come to leave it.

The good farmers' wives had welcomed us hospitably, the labouring women had grunted a greeting

as they trudged home with their loads, so did their little children along the road; Jacques from the mill, Jean from the farm, were all our acquaintances—the Laitière at her door, the friendly old grocers opposite the church.

I remember that one day a travelling organ came round to Visy, and was for half the day in the market-place grinding its tunes. The people inside the church could hear it. The old grocer's little granddaughters stood in the shop-door dancing and practising their steps; they were pretty little pensionnaires from the convent, with blue ribbons and medals like Pauline's tied round their necks. The old couple looked on, nodding their heads in time to the children.

"'They are beginning early," said the old lady, proudly; "they will be ready for the St. Côme." The St. Côme was an annual dance at Estournelles hard by, to which the whole village was looking forward. . .

Our lease had come to an end, and the house had to be given up to Madame Valmy, its rightful owner. A very grim-looking maid-servant came to receive the keys, and to take possession. All our own boxes and parcels were carried out through the garden, and placed ready in the road for the little omnibus. It ran daily past our gate at ten o'clock, and caught the early train to Paris from Corbeil. My luggage, however, was kept distinct from the family penates, and was piled up on a wheelbarrow, for the gardener to convey to the Château in the course of the morning.

I do not think I have described the Pavilion, as our house was called, now standing empty in the sunshine awaiting the return of its owner. Madame Valmy had put up at the little inn for the night, and was not to come in till the following day; but this maid-servant, Julienne, as they called her, had appeared early in the morning to go over the inventory, and to receive the keys from me, the only survivor of our cheerful colony. Julienne was not a pleasant person to have to do with. She was stout and pale, with a heavy sulky face. She seemed constantly suspecting me of some sinister purpose as she walked over the house, counted the inventory, and asked for the rent. Monsieur Fontaine had the rent. He had promised to get change for a cheque and to bring the amount, but Julienne did not seem to believe me when I told her so. The house stood at right angles between a garden and a courtyard; the drawing-room windows opened into the garden, the door of the house led to the courtyard; the courtyard opened into a side street of the village, so that there were two distinct entrances to the house.

People calling generally came through the court where the bell hung under a little tiled roof all to itself; but it was quite easy to open the garden gate if you knew the trick of the latch, and to come in by the drawing-room windows. An iron gateway, and wreathed by a vine, divided the courtyard from the garden. This door was always locked, besides which the vine had travelled on and on and bound the hinges and the iron scrolls together. I was standing in the courtyard that morning still talking to Julienne and trying to divert her many suspicions, when some shadow fell upon me, and turning round I saw that someone was looking at me through the grating. It was the figure of a slim woman in a pink dress, with a very bright complexion. In one hand she held a green parasol. She laid her white fingers upon the lock. "Madame, you know very well that there is no getting through that way," said Julienne. The woman's voice was singularly rough and yet distinct. As she spoke the figure disappeared. I don't know what it was that impressed me so disagreeably in both maid and mistress. It is difficult not to believe in some atmosphere which strangers coming into a place often feel, although they may not always understand it. Meanwhile Julienne went on with her investigations. "Where are the chests off the landing?" said she. "We put

them out of the way," I answered. "You will find
them in the little cellar off the dining-room." The
housekeeper was not satisfied until she had lighted
a candle, descended the three stone steps that led
to the cellar, and examined the locks, to make sure
they had not been tampered with. "There is another cellar beyond," said she, "but it is full of good
wine, and we did not give you the key."

I was not sorry when Pauline interrupted our
tête-à-tête; she had goodnaturedly come off to fetch
me. "Here you are, miss," she said. "I have been
to the station with papa. I saw your uncle and your
cousins go off, and now you belong to me for ever
so long;" and she took my hands in hers and shook
them cordially. Her eyes looked very bright, and
her hair very curly. "Well, have you nearly done?
can you come with me? How are you? How is
your mistress, Julienne, and when is the wedding
to be?"

Julienne answered drily that she never asked
questions, and that if people were curious they had
better enquire for themselves. Pauline turned away
with the family shrug. "The longer it is put off the
better pleased I shall be," she said. "I can't imagine
how she can think of him. The English are so
ridiculous. I wouldn't marry an Englishman."

I was little more than a schoolgirl, and my

temper was already roused. "I think it is very rude, and unkind, and inhospitable of you, if you are my friend, to talk in this dreadful way," I cried, almost with tears in my eyes. "The English are not ridiculous, they are a noble——"

"Do you really mind what I say," said Pauline, taking my hand. "Please, my dear friend, forgive me," and she looked at me full of concern, so that I was obliged to laugh.

Then, as soon as she had made sure I had forgiven her she walked out of the house. Pauline did not look round to see whether I had followed her out, pushed open the door of the courtyard, and marched out into the street. She was very rude at times, and made me more angry than anybody else, but she was so kind and feeling too that I always forgave her. My own cousins were gay, gentle, friendly in manner; she was either quite silent, or she would talk by the hour. She was alternately dull and indifferent and boisterous in her mirth; she was by way of hating affectation, and of thinking everybody affected; in order to show how sincere she was, she seemed to go out of her way to invent rudenesses. She was not even pretty. She might have had a good complexion but for her freckles; a pretty smile and white teeth seemed to be her only attraction. As I have said, she generally wore an

ill-made green frock, country shoes, and coarse
knitted stockings. Till she was sixteen she had
persisted in keeping her petticoats half up to her
knees, with black stuff trousers, such as girls wore in
those days, and a black stuff apron and sleeves to
match.

"No," said Pauline, again, "I cannot think how
my pretty delightful Madame Valmy can think of
marrying your Capitaine Thomsonne, or how she can
keep that horrid Julienne in her service."

As she spoke we were passing Fontaine's house,
and his head appeared for one instant in a window;
the next minute he had hurried into the road to
greet us. "Are you aware that Madame Valmy is
come?" he said, in great excitement. "I have just
seen Le Capitaine, who seems a little suffering. But
our fine air will set him up. I am immediately
starting to pay my respects to Madame. I hope,
Mademoiselle Pauline, with your leave, that our
musical evenings at the Château will now recom-
mence, the prima donna being among us once more.
To-morrow I am engaged upon business for my
friend Monsieur Mérard, but Thursday we might all
combine perhaps."

"I will let you know," said Pauline. "We may
be busy." She spoke with some constraint. The
Maire gave one rapid glance.

It is strange what a part in life the things play which never happen. We think of them and live for them, and they form a portion of our history, and while we are still absorbed in these imaginary dreams the realities of our lives meet us on the way, and we suddenly awaken to the truth at last. Pauline thought that her fate was being decided, and that by Thursday all secret destinies were to be unravelled; no wonder that she was silent as we walked along.

CHAPTER IV.

MADEMOISELLE PAULINE'S MARRIAGE PORTION.

WHEN the Comte de Mesnil fell into that hopeless condition from which he never rallied, but sank after some months of illness, it was found that his affairs were in utter confusion. He had kept his difficulties secret even from his wife. It was impossible to tell whether this impending ruin had produced the mental disturbance from which he was suffering, or whether the ruin had not been partly owing to some secret want of balancing power; for his extravagance had been almost without a limit. The Countess had tried in the first years of their marriage to interfere; but for long past had forborne to blame her husband or to enquire into his affairs. She herself had drawn largely upon his resources. To do him justice, the Count was indifferent to money for its own sake, and had only been anxious that everyone should be as comfortable as circumstances might admit. Unfortunately one day came when circumstances no longer admitted of any comfort for anybody. The Count's creditors seized his great house in Paris; the sheriff's officers were in possession; the whole magnificent apparatus of damask, and crystal, and china was to be disposed of by public auction. And the unfortunate Countess, who was more difficult to dispose of, was sitting, silent, resentful, and offended beyond words or the power of words, in a temporary lodging which her son had taken for her use. She had a daughter also, an amiable and gentle girl, who tried in vain to console her, for Madame de Mesnil looked upon all attempts at consolation as insults. We have seen how she treated M. Fontaine. Maurice her son, now Comte de Mesnil in his own right, had suggested their all going into the country, and trying to live as economically as might be upon what might remain to them; but even this moderate scheme was not to be carried out. The estate at Visy remained, but there was scarcely anything left besides, and the only thing to be done was to sell that too and to live upon the proceeds of the sale. The one piece of good fortune which befell this unfortunate family was the advent of a purchaser for the estate. This was our friend Fournier, who was willing to pay a fair price for the land and the old house upon it. He produced certain sums of money representing a great deal of good sense, hard work, and self-denial, and received in return the estate which the late Count's folly and self-indulgence had thrown into the market.

Maurice had several interviews with the old manufacturer—ventured to make one or two suggestions about the management of the property, which had been very ill received by his late father, but which nevertheless were, in Fournier's opinion, worth considering. Something in the young Count's manner, his courtesy and simplicity of bearing, impressed the old man in his favour. Fournier thought himself no bad judge of character, and after that little talk with Pauline he made up his mind. He cared less for money than people usually do who have not earned it. It seemed to him that there were other things wanting besides money to make his girl happy in her marriage. "This young fellow is clear-headed, modest, ready to occupy himself intelligently; he will make an excellent landlord. My wife has a fancy to see a countess's coronet on her daughter's pocket-handkerchief. Pauline might do worse," he said to Fontaine. "I am going to Paris to-morrow to speak to the Baron. That is an old fox if you like, but I like the young man."

"I have known Maurice from his childhood," said Fontaine, solemnly (so he told me afterwards); "he is a gallant man, incapable of a dishonourable action. I will answer for him with my word and——"

"Good, good, good," says Fournier, who hated phrases. "I daresay he is very like other people; it will be a good business for him. My Pauline, and my rent-roll, and my share in the factory—it is not a bad bargain he will make."

It was the very day I went up to stay at the house that Fournier came back from Paris, having concluded this solemn affair.

We had been walking in the park, in silence, for Pauline seemed absent, and for once she did not care to go on with her usual somewhat long-winded histories. There is a little mound near the terrace from whence one can see the road winding between its poplars, the great fields lying one beyond the other, some golden with corn, others black with peat and with smoking heaps, of which the vapours drifted along the horizon. "There is my father coming," cried Pauline suddenly, and she started running along the avenue, and came up to M. Fournier just at the entrance gate by the poplar-trees, of which all the shadows seemed to invite the passing wayfarers to come in and rest. I followed, running too, because Pauline ran. I am afraid it showed small discretion on my part.

"Well, Pauline," said her father kindly, stopping to breathe. Then he turned to me. "How do you do, miss? I am glad to see you."

"Where have you been, papa; what have you been about?" Pauline said, after a minute of silence.

"I have had a hard day's work in your service," he answered. "I have been to call upon M. le Baron de Beaulieu, upon Madame la Comtesse de Mesnil," said the father, stroking her check with his finger. "I have been working for you, mademoiselle. I hope it is all for the best," he repeated, with a sigh. "Mr. Maurice seems a fine young fellow. I do not like the mother."

"Don't you, papa?" said Pauline, absently; and she stooped and pulled up a handful of grass, which she then blew away into the air.

"To be Madame la Comtesse is small comfort where hearts are cold, and the home an empty lonely place," said Fournier. "Well, well, the young man is coming here as you wish. You must see him and make up your mind. I don't think he can ever learn how to love you, my child, as well as your old father does." Fournier was very gentle and sad, and he went on swinging his stick, and said no more. I lingered behind and watched the father and daughter walk away together, up the avenue towards the house, trudging along side by side, looking strangely alike. When I came in Pauline was not to be seen. M. Fournier was sitting reading the paper in his usual corner. Madame Fournier met me on the stairs; I think she had been crying. She stopped me. "Do not go to Pauline just yet," she said; "she is agitated, dear child—she——we——. Monsieur Fournier has decided. I have been very happy myself," she added, with a tender look in her flushed red face; "I should like my child to know such happiness. M. de Mesnil is coming here to-morrow."

They were good and worthy people. I was glad to be with them.

I was happy enough up at the Château, but I could imagine that for a young man it might seem rather monotonous at times. Maurice used to think it almost unbearably so in his father's time, and secretly hated the place. One cannot reason out every motive which prompts each human action. Sufficient be it if the sum, on the whole, drives the impulse rightly. Perhaps it had been no great sacrifice to the young man to hear that the cruel fates had exiled him from this dreary, familiar, wearisome old home, and that he was to return thither no more. Long after he confessed everything to Pauline; and the dismay he felt when his mother sent for him, and with happy agitation told him of the wonderful chance by which, if he was so inclined, the old home might return to its ancient possessors, to the owners whose right she still considered greater than that of mere purchase. As Maurice heard for the first time of his uncle's suggestion and Fournier's acquiescence, his heart only sank lower and lower; his mother's delight and eager exclamations sounded like a knell to his hopes. "And now, now," cried the poor lady, exulting, "I shall not die with the bitter pang in my heart that your father's was the hand which exiled my son from the home to which he had a right; now," she said, "my life will close peacefully, reassured for my children's fate. My daughter need not fear the future. Your home will be hers at my death. I have not deserved so much; it makes up to me for my life of anxious sorrow," said the poor lady, bursting into tears, and covering her face with her hands. Poor Maurice knew not how to answer. His heart went on sinking and sinking; it had leapt up at the prospect of liberty, of hard work, of change, of independence. He had behaved very well; but he had been doing as he liked for the first time in all his life, and now more firmly than ever did the fetters seem rivetted which were to bind him down to Visy. The black canals seemed to rise and rise and choke him; the dreary old gables seemed to weigh upon his very soul. For a few moments he stood silent, making up his mind. He was trying to frame the scentence by which to explain to his mother what he felt.

"'There is much to be considered," he was beginning. Then she raised her head; her entreating eyes met his, she put up her thin hands.

"Oh, my son!" she said. "Do you think I sacrifice nothing when I give you up to strangers, that my mother's pride does not suffer at the thought of this cruel necessity? My Maurice, you have been my consolation and my courage; and oh, believe me, my son, you will never regret the impulse which makes you yield to your mother's prayer. Think what my life has been, think of the sorrows I have hidden from my children. Ah! do not condemn me to that renewed penance; I have no more strength for it." She put her arms round his neck with tender persistence. Her wasted looks, her tears, and above all her tenderness, which he had so often longed for as a child, and which had been so rarely expressed, overcame the poor kind-hearted young fellow's faint effort at resistance. He turned very pale, his lips seemed quite dry and parched, and something seemed to impede his speech as he said, "Very well. Since you wish it, I will consent. The sooner it is all settled the better, I suppose." He shook off little Claudine, who came coaxing up to him with innocent congratulations. He scarcely answered his uncle's long speeches and elaborations, when the Baron arrived in his black satin stock, prepared to undertake any negotiations. Three days later, Maurice went down to Visy. From a French point of view, the whole thing was a highly desirable and honourable proceeding. M. le Comte de Mesnil arrived in a dogged and determined state of mind, prepared to go through with the dreary farce.

CHAPTER V.

MADEMOISELLE PAULINE'S INTENDED HUSBAND.

IT must have seemed like a sort of mockery to poor Maurice to see the familiar chairs in the hall, to hear the well-known tick of the old clock in the great salon, and to be solemnly announced to the company assembled at the Château—M. Fournier, Madame Fournier, Pauline with her Sunday frock, and Fontaine the friend of the family, who had been invited to break the formality of this first introduction. M. de Mesnil was a youth of the usual type, with honest grey eyes, not unlike Pauline's. He was pale, slight, distinguished in manner and appearance—a contrast to the worthy master of the house, in which M. Fournier certainly seemed to me very much out of place. Pauline looked very pale, too, very clumsy, but noble, somehow, notwithstanding her plaid frock and her twists. Maurice was perfectly quiet and conventional, bowed with his hat in his hand, expressed his gratitude for the invitation he had received, sat down in a company attitude upon the old armchair against which he had so often knocked his nose as a child. He took Madame Fournier into dinner, Pauline sat on his other hand. They had a melon, soup, sweetbreads, a gigot, with a plated handle to carve it by; a round tart, cream-cheese, and champagne for dessert. "The dinner was excellent, but Maurice certainly did not distinguish himself," the Maire observed. "I did my best, but conversation languished."

For the first few days M. de Mesnil was busy with his father-in-law going over the estate and the business connected with it, and while he had work to do, Maurice seemed comparatively resigned; but when, on the third morning, M. Fournier told him to go in and make himself agreeable to his wife and daughter, Maurice felt the old dismay return tenfold. He had little in common with the ladies. He might respect Pauline, but he was certainly afraid of her; and as for making himself agreeable, nothing seemed left for him to do but wander vapidly about from one room to another, or to saunter along the terrace with Pauline and with Madame Fournier, who conscientiously and laboriously chaperoned the couple. One day I found him yawning in the hall, and watching the darning of stockings. Another day he assisted Pauline with the garden-roller. Pauline was a curiously determined person. She would not give up one of her pursuits for any number of aspirants. "Let them come, too," said she, "if they want to see me." Some horrible dulness overpowered Maurice; a nightmare seemed to be upon the place, and Pauline was only a part of it, and so was everything else. Formerly he used to have schemes for benefiting the tenants, now he no longer wished to benefit anybody. Once it seemed to him want of funds which prevented his efforts— now it was some strange inability to do and care and to interest himself which had come over him: they had taken his liberty away, condemned him to a life he was weary of. He did not care what happened.

He took us out in a punt one day; and I remember when we ran aground it was Pauline, not Maurice, who sprang into the water and pushed us off.

Madame Fournier screamed. M. Fournier only laughed. Pauline, shaking her wet clothes, said it was nothing. However, she conceded something to de Mesnil's well-bred concern, and went back to the house to change her wet things. Maurice would have accompanied her, but his father-in-law called him back.

"Let her be, let her be! She will be quicker without you. We shall meet her at the little bridge." Then we went on our way again in the punt, rather a silent party. The banks slide by, so do the stumps, and the willow rods starting from among the up-springing weeds, and grasses and water-plants stream upon the waters. How dark and blue the sky looked overhead, studding the pale green of the willow-trees!

"That naughty child!" said Madame Fournier. "She will get some frightful illness one day if she is not more careful. I am glad you persuaded her to change her wet things, M. Maurice. She would not have done it for me."

"In my time," said old Fournier, "it was the young men, not the young women, who jumped into the water. You have certainly not brought your daughter up to think of the *bienséances*, Louise."

"It is not my doing, Monsieur Fournier," said his wife, reddening. "You would never allow me to hold her back. How many times have I not——"

"Good, good, good!" cries M. Fournier, in his irritated voice. "This is the hundredth time you tell me all this."

I saw Maurice bite his lip while this discussion was going on. He did not speak; he continued to work the long pole by which we were shoved along; the boat steadily progressed, rounded the point, came out into a sudden glow of light, air, sunshine.

There was the bridge, there was a sight of the old house with its many windows. Three figures were standing by the bridge. Pauline herself, still in her wet clothes, a short little gentleman with a moustache, and a tall lady waving a green parasol.

"Who is it?" says Fournier, blinking.

"Why, here is Madame Valmy!" cried Madame Fournier, quite pleased, and bristling up with conscious maternal excitement at the news she had to give. "And Pauline——"

Mademoiselle Fournier turned and nodded to us. She was wet, soiled, splashed from head to foot. She was talking eagerly to the friends she had encountered, to the flourishing little gentleman, to the elegant lady, curled, trimmed, cool, in perfect order, who seemed to me to give a sarcastic little glance every now and then at poor Pauline's drenched garments. Fournier called out very angrily again, why had she waited, why had she not gone home?

"I am going, papa. They did not know the way," shouted Pauline. And she set off, running and swinging her arms as she went along. Then Fournier, rather reluctantly I thought, greeted his guests. Madame Valmy was invited into the punt by Madame Fournier.

"Get in, if you like," said Fournier. "There will be room enough. You can take my place. I will show the captain my new hydraulic pump, if he will walk across with me to the stables."

It was a curious change of atmosphere when, with a rustle and a gentle half-toned laugh, Madame Valmy stepped into the broad boat, and settled herself down beside me. I saw Maurice looking at her with some surprise. She was smiling. To-day she wore a blue gown, and falling muslin sleeves and ruffles. She held her ivory parasol daintily in one mittened hand; she laughed, talked, seemed at once to become one with us all. It was certainly a great relief to the poor young Count to meet this fascinating, agreeable, fashionable person in his somewhat wearisome Arcadia. His eyes brightened, some change came over him; and Madame Sidonie herself, as she liked to be called, appeared greatly interested by the melancholy, pale, romantic looks of M. de Mesnil. She opened her eyes, seemed to understand everything in a minute, and I could read her amused surprise that Pauline, of all people in the world, should have discovered such a husband. Nothing would content Madame Fournier but that Madame Valmy should return to the Château with us. The two gentlemen were pacing the terrace and tranquilly discussing pumps. Pauline came to meet us along the avenue, and all the fragrant darkness seemed to me like a tide rising among the

stems of the trees. The house-door was open wide.
The hall was lighted with two oil lamps; a tray
with various cordials and glasses stood on the
billiard-table.

"Come in and rest," said Pauline. "Won't you
have some beer, instead of all this?"

Madame Valmy laughed and shrank back;
Pauline tossed off a glass; and Fontaine now appeared from within; he had been tuning his fiddle
in the drawing-room, and the candles were already
lighted on the piano.

Although Madame Valmy refused the beer, she
accepted a glass of chartreuse, and then consented
to open the concert, and to sit down at the piano,
and to sing a romance which made Maurice thrill
again. It was something about—

> Je suis triste—je voudrais mou-ri-re,
> Car j'ai perdue—ue, mon ami,
> La la la la li-re.

. When she had finished, M. le Maire accompanied
Mademoiselle Fournier on his violin all through an
immensely long piece of music, so difficult that he
declared no amateur would ever be able to master
it, and during the performance of which the Intended
was busy paying compliments and whispering remarks to the songstress. My attention wandered

away to the two as they sat on the big couch by the window, while the Maire went on from one agonising passage to another, beating time with his foot, running frantic scales, and poor Pauline, with her elbows squared, was banging away at the piano, and rumbling in the bass so as to imitate thunder. She had put on a dress, with two frills sticking up on the shoulders. Her mouth was open, her eyes fixed on her music, her tight bronze shoes hard at work at the pedals. Madame Fournier was in her chair delightedly nodding time. M. Fournier in the distance reading the paper by the light of a lamp with a green shade. M. de Mesnil looked away from his bride and her surroundings to the charming lady who was glancing so archly at him over her waving fan. No wonder if he sighed and thought, perhaps, that honest Pauline was not exactly the idea which a young man would dream of at his start in life—the sympathetic being who, &c. &c. &c. But meanwhile squeak-eak goes the fiddle, bang, rumble, bang goes Pauline, and Sidonie Valmy's deep eyes are glancing, her glittering fan waves faintly, her silence says a thousand things, her smiles sing siren songs, and the foolish young man is sinking, sinking, head over ears in the deep water.

CHAPTER VI.

MADAME VALMY.

AFTER all these romances and minor chords, my conversation with Madame Valmy that night before she went home seemed rather a come down to commonplace again. She came up very graciously to speak to me as I sat in my corner. She seemed in high spirits, with pink cheeks blushing.

"I am now at home, and I have to thank your uncle for the rent which he left with M. Fontaine," she said. "My maid, Julienne, who is very difficult to please, tells me that your servants have left everything in excellent condition. She begged me to ask," said Madame, with a charming smile, "if you happened to know anything of the key of the door to the recess in the dining-room. We keep our provisions there, the place is so cool and dark—I am giving so much trouble, but Therese is dreadfully particular . . . ."

De Mesnil prepared to walk home with our visitors across the park. Pauline said she should also like to accompany them. It was quite dark, but she came back alone whistling and calling to her dog.

"I sent him on to the village, mama," she said, in answer to Madame Fournier's glance. "Mary is coming with me for another stroll." She took my hand and held it tight in hers. As we walked out into the evening once more everything looked weird and shadowy, but the last twilight gleam was still in the sky. Pauline did not look up; she was thinking of other things, her heart was full and she wanted to speak; she suddenly began in a low moved voice. "Ah!" she said, "what a great responsibility is another person's happiness! How do I know that I can make him happy? Of what use would it be to me to be Madame la Comtesse? Of what use would the park, and all the trees, and the houses and furniture, and all my money, be to M. Maurice if he was not happy? I am foolish," she said. "I don't know what I want. Mama had only seen my father once when she agreed to marry him. Maurice is so different. His habits are not like mine. Oh! I think I could not, could not bear it, if I thought he was unhappy with me. But my father and mother must know better than I can do. They have judged wisely for me in their tender affection, and I can abide by their decision."

We had come to the gate in the wall; it had

been left wide open; I passed out and looked out across the fields.

"Do you see him coming?" said Pauline. "Shall we wait here a little bit?"

We waited a very long time, but Maurice did not come. It was not till I was undressed that I heard the hall-door unbarred, and M. Fournier's voice as he let the young man in.

It was a hot sultry night, and I could not sleep. I went to the window of my room, which looked out at the back of the house into the park. A sort of almost supernatural sweetness seemed brooding from the vaguely illumined sky, where one great dewy planet hung sparkling. The other stars were dimmed by this wonderful radiance. The cattle were out in the dark fields beyond the trees, and from time to time I heard them lowing. The sound came distinct, and sounded melodious, somehow, and reassuring. Everything was still and very hot. Strange vaporous things whirled past me in the darkness. Moths beat their gauzy sails. Was it a bat's wing that flapped across the beautiful star, as I leant from the window, breathing in the fragrant perfume of some creeper that was nailed against the wall? I could see a line of light from Pauline's window, shooting out into the darkness. Then I saw, vaguely at first, and then more distinctly, some shadowy movement among the flower-beds at the end of the paved terrace. Then the shadow seemed to gain in substance and form, and the sound of slow falling footsteps reached me. I was only a girl, and superstitious still in those days, and for a moment my heart beat fast. But almost immediately I recognised something familiar in the movement which told me that it was the very substantial figure of M. Fournier that was wandering in and out and round and about the little flower-beds. It seemed to me a strange proceeding on his part, for it was not the beauty of the night which attracted him. As he passed my window, he seemed to me muttering angrily to himself. "Que diable!" I heard him say. Then I went to sleep, and awoke with a start, still listening to the wandering footsteps. After all his talk about early hours, here was M. Fournier himself restlessly pacing the night away.

Captain Thompson was very much occupied just about this time. He was winding up some affairs connected with another peat factory which he had started at Estournelles. He used to be absent all day, and only came in late in time for dinner. He was not there to turn over Madame Valmy's pages as she sat at her piano on the hot autumnal afternoons, but somehow de Mesnil was always ready to do her errands, or to wait her orders. Pauline was not a severe taskmistress, and never attempted to keep him by her side when he wished to go.

Monsieur Fontaine, who did not deny having been himself very much attracted by the lovely widow, shook his head solemnly, and disapproved exceedingly of her flirtation with Maurice de Mesnil. Rarer and rarer were the accompaniments his fiddle scraped to Madame Valmy's love ditties, but the songstress somehow thrilled on. Day after day de Mesnil would come sauntering down the street, and stop and go in at the gateway of the Pavilion, and the performance would presently begin, and the music would come floating across the court.

Pauline herself was an odd mixture of simplicity and shrewdness, and she went about loudly professing her admiration for the son-in-law her father had chosen. De Mesnil's refinement, his gentleness, impressed the brusque young bourgeoise with a certain shy admiring respect. She declared that he was too good for her, that he was throwing himself away; that she expected some obstacle must intervene. She was a girl of singular frankness—she never said a word that was not truth itself. She hated exaggeration; she had no sense of humour; her frankness was sometimes objectionable, her remarks stupid and ill-timed, and yet, in common with all conscientious persons, there was a certain

force of character about her which impressed those
who came in contact with her. Her mother always
ended by succumbing; her father, from whom she
inherited this turn of mind, generally ended by giving in to her wishes.

It was not to be supposed that if Fontaine's eyes
were open hers were closed, and that if the Maire
had commented upon what was passing she too did
not suffer some natural pangs of jealousy.

Fontaine thought it his duty to speak to M.
Fournier on the subject—so he told me confidentially; but the retired manufacturer stopped him at
once.

"I have promised Pauline not to interfere for
the present," said he; "I can trust her good sense.
You will be helping me most effectually by saying
no more on this subject to me or to anyone else."

"Of course I can only respect his wishes," said
Fontaine; and so I told Mademoiselle Pauline, and
so M. Fontaine told me whenever an opportunity
occurred.

The key which Madame Valmy had asked me
for was not to be found. My cousin wrote, and
Pauline and I went one day to the village locksmith, and ordered another in its place.

"Madame Valmy's Julienne has already been
here to tell me to make one," said Leroux, the

locksmith. "She desired me to send you the account."

Madame Coqueau, the locksmith's mother-in-law, who was the village newsmonger, here chimed in. "The Captain's cider and champagne had arrived," she said; "no wonder they were in want of a key; and that Julienne, for all her grim airs, was as fond of a bottle of good wine as others with half her pretensions."

Madame Coqueau evidently shared my dislike to Julienne. Pauline and I said good-bye to Madame Coqueau, good-day to the Curé, whom we passed. We were walking home leisurely up the street, chattering and looking about; I had just asked where the Captain was living, when we passed a low white house, covered with a trellis.

"This is his house," said Pauline, "and that is the Doctor's opposite."

Then we came to the gates of the Pavilion, which were open, for Captain Thompson was crossing the courtyard from the house. He was looking very smiling and trim as usual. He took off his hat when he saw us, stopped, and came up to Pauline, saying—

"I was just going in search of a good-natured person, mademoiselle. Would you consent to do me a favour? Fontaine has been drawing up a

paper for me. Sidonie can't sign, because she is
interested. We want someone to witness my signature, and if you young ladies would be so kind as
to come in for one minute, everything would be en
reggel. This is very good of you," as he stood by
to let us pass. We went up the steps and past the
kitchen. Julienne was standing at the door with a
saucepan in her hand. Pauline said "Good morning," but Julienne did not answer. She looked as
if she would have liked to throw her saucepan at
our heads. I could not imagine what we had done
to vex her.

"You must not mind her," said Captain Thompson, as we came into the dining-room. "She is in
one of her ill-humours. Only Sidonie, who is
sweetness itself, would put up with her. She is
rude to everyone. She positively refused to witness for us just now, and that is why I have to
trouble you, ladies." Then he opened the drawing-
room door and ushered us in. Sidonie, in her
sweetest temper and blue trimmings, was installed
in her big soft chair by the window. She seemed
unprepared for our appearance, but her embarass-
ment did not last.

"Well, Sid! here are some witnesses," said the
Captain; "now we shall get the business settled."

A huge foolscap lay on the table, emblazoned

in Gothic letters with "Will of Captain J. Beauvoir Thompson, of Amphlett Hall, Lancaster." M. Fontaine was writing something at a side-table. He waved his hand to us and went on.

Captain Thompson went up and read over Fontaine's shoulder, while I looked round in some surprise. Was this the room we had lived in for so many months? It seemed transformed into some strange place. The furniture was differently arranged, dark blinds had been put up in the windows, mirrors hung from the walls; bonbon boxes, footstools were scattered all about, huge japan pots stood on the chimney; some sense of enclosure had come over the place; there was a faint scent of patchouli, a log was smouldering in the grate. The homely country fragrance of the vines and the garden-beds had pleased me better on the whole.

"There," said the Captain, as Fontaine finished. "Thank you, Fongtaine, and now, in case of anything happening to me between this and the weddin', I shall feel sure that you won't be put upon, my poor little woman. I know I'm absurd, but——" he walked across to where Madame Valmy was sitting.

She did not notice him at first. "Why do you persist in dwelling upon such dreadful thoughts?" said she, starting up suddenly with a glance at

Pauline; "why trouble yourself about me; I should manage somehow, anyhow, as I did before I knew you. What should I want else if I had not my foolish, foolish——"

Here she pulled out her handkerchief.

"There, there, don't cry, dear; it is all non-sense," said he. "You get anxious, you silly child," and his voice softened. "Why, it was something you said yourself last night which put it all into my head. It is only a fancy. I shan't die any the sooner for writing my name upon a piece of paper."

As he walked back to the table, the door opened and Julienne looked in. He was deliberately writing his name with a flourish; Madame Valmy was watching him, and I, looking up, saw Julienne's strange eyes reflected in the glass. Then Pauline witnessed the signature; and as she, too, suddenly met this strange fixed glance she turned pale.

"What is it, Julienne?" said she. "Why do you look at me like that?"

Julienne gave no answer, but walked away.

Madame Valmy began to laugh, rather hysterically. "I don't know what is the matter with Julienne," said she; "she seems to have a horror of business. I myself am rather interested in it."

"Business! Sid thinks she understands about

business!" said the Captain, fondly. "Shall I tell Fongtaine what a confusion you had got into, poor child, when you first consulted me? Think of her trying to speculate at the Bourse."

Madame Valmy, with burning cheeks, was evidently vexed by the conversation, and the good Captain saw this and became serious at once.

"Thank'ee, thank'ee," he said, folding up the slips and putting them neatly away in his despatch-box.

The incident was slight enough, but it made an impression on me. I remembered his kind look afterwards.

"You English," said Fontaine, gathering up his hat and gloves; "you are a generous, impulsive race. I am sure, M. le Capitaine, that Madame Valmy must be touched by your care for her."

"Nonsense, nonsense," said the Captain. "Sid makes a great deal out of nothing. Now then, Julienne and I are going to put by the cider. I believe that is the real secret of her impatience this morning. Good-bye, thank you," he repeated.

Madame also accompanied us to the door, waving farewells. She embraced Pauline, who seemed to me less demonstrative than she had usually been to her friend. She did not say a single word as we walked away. At the end of the village street, by the church, we met Maurice walking down.

"Were you coming to meet us?" Pauline asked, brightening up when she saw him.

He looked at her gravely, and said, "No, I was not, but I will walk back with you if you will allow me."

He and Pauline went first; I followed. I could not help, as I went along, speculating about Madame Valmy and her feeling for the Captain. It seemed to me that it was *Fontaine* who had been touched by the Captain's affection for Madame Valmy, far more than that lady herself, for she certainly was not crying when she pulled out her handkerchief.

————

CHAPTER VII.

COFFEE.

ENGLISH Parisians are a curious race of willing
exiles from their own country. I remember how I
and my companions as girls used to feel an odd
isolation at times and shame for our expatriation.
We used to hang up our youthful harps by the
waters of Babylon and lament our captivity, and
think with longing of the green pastures and still
waters of our native land.   Older people feel things
differently. Captain Thompson for one was never so
well pleased as when anybody mistook him and his
paddings and his blue boots for a Frenchman.   He
was respected in his own country; he was the master
of a pretty home there and a comfortable estate;
but his dream was to live abroad, and to be ordered
about by the widow.   He would have changed his
name, and his nationality, if he could, as he did his
clothes, and all his habits, soon after making Madame Valmy's acquaintance.   After he knew her
time and space were not, except indeed so far as

they concerned her and her wishes. For two years
he had lived in her presence; he had taught himself
French, which he spoke with wonderful fluency and
an inaccuracy which was almost heroic. Madame
Valmy used to stop her pretty little ears at times;
the Captain would blush, try to correct himself good-
humouredly, and go on again, after gallantly kissing
her fair hand by way of making peace. Of his
devotion to her there was little doubt; her feelings
for him used often to puzzle me. She seemed to
avoid his company, to be bored by him; to accept
his devotion, his care, his romance, with weariness
and impatience. I have seen a doubtful look in his
honest round face at times, and then at a word from
her, some friendly little sign, he would brighten up
again.

Little girls who are not yet of an age to be
engrossed in conversation or in their own affairs are
more observant than people imagine, and although
Pauline praised Madame Valmy from morning to
night, I never heartily responded. She was white,
she was pink, she was exquisitely dressed, she was
kind, her eyes were blue under her thick fair eyebrows; but it seemed to me that her kindness, her
grace, her soft colours, were not the spontaneous
outcomings of a gentle heart, but the deliberate
exertion of her wish to please, to seem charming to

certain persons for purposes of her own. It seemed
to me that she was stupid, and with all her clever-
ness devoid of imagination. I remember once seeing
her push a toddling child out of her way into the
gutter; the little thing fell and began to cry; Madame Valmy walked quietly on, scarcely glancing to
see whether the baby was hurt. It was Monsieur
Fontaine, who happened to be on his doorstep, who
came down, picked the child up, and gave it a sugarplum, and wiped its face with his bandanna handkerchief.

Madame Valmy had been spoiled all her life, by
fortune, by misfortune, by trouble of every kind.
She had married to escape a miserable home, but
she married a rough and jealous and brutal man,
whom she had never loved, and his cruelty roused
all that was worst in her nature. Madame Valmy
seemed to be utterly without the gift of conscience.
Some people are said not to have souls—at least
that is the only way in which I can account for
events which came to my knowledge afterwards, and
which never seemed to me quite satisfactorily explained away. Sometimes I believe for a minute
some vague vision of better things than her own
warmth and ease and greed and need for admiration
would come before her, but these visions were only
passing ones; at the first nip of cold, the first effort

of self-restraint, this weak, stubborn, reckless creature forgot everything but her own grasping wishes—to be first, to be rich, envied, admired, to dazzle and eclipse all other women, to fascinate every man within her reach, to go to heaven charming M. le Curé and M. le Vicaire by the way—I can hardly tell what she hoped and what she did not hope. She was not grateful, for she took everything as her due, while she had the bitter resentments of a person who over-estimates her own consequence; but with all this her manner was so charming, so gentle and sprightly, her laughter was so sympathetic, her allusions to her past sufferings so natural and so simple, that most people were utterly convinced by her. Madame Fournier and Pauline both thought there was no one like their pretty, poor, ill-used Madame Valmy. Fournier mistrusted her, but Fontaine would have gone to the farthest end of his Commune for her, and as for our compatriot Captain Thompson, he was head and ears in love with her, and considered himself engaged to the sweetest angel in the world.

He had first known her at Visy in her husband's lifetime; it was from Valmy that he had bought his land and the little house in the village which he inhabited. Captain Thompson never spoke of those days. I have seen him turn quite pale when Fontaine made any allusion to the time when they first met. Fontaine was less sensitive, and used to give us dark hints of Madame Valmy's history. I remember one evening, as we were all strolling across the fields in the sunset, that Fontaine was discoursing about the Valmy *ménage* and stove in his dining-room.

"It is six years since it was put up," said he. "I remember that the only civility the late M. Valmy ever showed me was at that time. He came to see it fixed and gave me several very useful hints."

"M. Valmy! You knew him then. What sort of man was he?" said Madame Fournier.

"That would not be very easy to tell you," said Fontaine. "He was a man of military carriage, bronze complexion, a black, penetrating eye, a taciturn disposition. You may have heard how he locked himself up, and his wife too for the matter of that. They say he once kept her for a whole month in one of those little cells out of the dining-room."

"Who says so?" cried a voice at our shoulder. What a horror! It was Pauline who had joined us.

"Ah, Mademoiselle!" said Fontaine; "excuse my

starting—in reply to your question," and he lowered his voice, "Madame Picard mentioned the circumstance to me. She lived next door, and she heard it from a servant who was soon afterwards dismissed."

"I don't believe it," said Pauline. "M. Fontaine, you should not repeat such things." All the same I saw Pauline watching Madame Valmy that evening with strange looks of pity. Well, her troubles were over. Captain Thompson seemed to be of quite a different temperament from his predecessor, and his one regret was that there were not more families in the neighbourhood with whom there was any possibility of intimacy. The retired pastrycook in the house near the church was scarcely an associate for educated people; the doctor was a stupid little being, born in the village, and with but two ideas in his head. One was that Madame Picard should look kindly on his suit, and join her fortune and her cows to his practice; the other idea was that an 'infusion de thé' was a specific for every malady.

On this particular evening, as we walked through the village, Madame Valmy began to ask us all in, to drink coffee in her garden.

"It is absurd," said she, "of me to invite you

down from your pleasant terrace to my little parterre, but, as you are here, if you will come in, the
Captain shall make the coffee. Nobody understands
the art so well as he does. Even Julienne admits
his superiority."

As she spoke she led the way and we all followed
one by one. We came in across the court-yard,
passed through the house and out into the garden
again, where a table was ready laid, and some
chairs were set out. Julienne, looking as black as
usual, and not prepared to admit anybody's superiority, came and went with coffee-cups and plates
of biscuit and cakes, clanking her wooden shoes.
The sky was ablaze, and so were the Michaelmas
daisies in Madame Valmy's flower-beds. They seemed
burning with most sweet and dazzling colour. A
glow of autumn spread over the walls and the vines,
and out beyond the grated door that looked upon
the road and the stubble-fields.

As I sat there I looked back into the comfortable
house through the drawing-room windows. M. Fontaine's dark inuendoes seemed utterly out of place
amid so much elegant comfort. How impossible
crime and sorrow seem when the skies are peacefully
burning, when the evil and the good are alike resting and enjoying the moment of tranquil ease! The

Captain may have been enjoying himself, but he
was not resting. He came and went, puffing and
hospitable, with a huge coffee-pot, from which he
filled our cups.

"Prengar, mon fille," he said to the maid-servant,
over whom he nearly tumbled once, coffee-pot and
all, in his eagerness to serve us. Pauline put out
her hand—one of the small tables went over;
Madame Valmy gave a little scream of annoyance, the hot milk was spilt over her pale azure
dress.

"Sidonie! my dear Sidonie, are you hurt?" cried
he.

She laughed, but it was an angry laugh. "I am
not in the least hurt, it is nothing," she said. "You
have only spoilt my dress, you or whoever it was,"
and the gleam of her blue eyes seemed to say, Pauline, you have done it on purpose. "Here, Julienne!
bring a handkerchief," she said; "there is one in my
work-basket."

"I know, I saw it there," cried Maurice, eagerly
jumping and running into the house.

I thought Pauline looked a little surprised that
Maurice should be so much at home at the Pavilion
as to know the contents of Madame Valmy's work-

basket. She said nothing. Madame Fournier stared at the young man when he came back, and if Fontaine had not started some discussion about the length of time that coffee should be allowed to boil, I think we should none of us have spoken. Presently Fournier put his untasted cup down on the table, and looked up at the evening star which was twinkling over the garden wall.

"It is getting cold," he said. "My rheumatism will not let me sit still here any longer. Pauline, will you come for another walk?" said he, "so long as it is not in the direction of Etournelles; they have got their dance for the St. Come."

"Papa!" cried Pauline, "that is exactly where I want to go."

"Etournelles, is that where they are dancing?" said Maurice; "why should we not go? The Captain shall dance, and so will I, and here is our agile friend Fontaine," he added, laughing.

"I would go four miles to get out of their way," said Monsieur Fournier, impatiently.

It is all very well for people who have danced for years and years to all manner of tunes and jigs until they are tired, to walk away quietly. Pauline and I were young enough to feel our hearts beat more quickly when we heard the scraping of fiddle-strings; our limbs seemed to keep some secret time to the call of these homely instruments (how many measures are there not to which one would fain keep time while life endures!). Some melancholy strain had been sounding in Pauline's ears as she sat among Madame Valmy's gay flower-beds. The thought of the peasants' dance at Etournelles came to her, I could plainly see, as a distraction, a means of escape from oppressing thoughts.

"Dear papa," said she, "let us go; take mamma home. Maurice is here, he and Monsieur Fontaine will see us back."

"And I may be allowed surely to chaperone the young ladies. They would enjoy the dance of all things," said Madame Valmy, recovering her temper.

But Madame Fournier objected, as any properly-educated French mother would be sure to do. Pauline must not be seen in public without her. What was Madame Valmy thinking of? To everybody's amazement Madame Fournier actually proposed to walk another mile to the dancing place. "M. Fournier, *thou* wilt send back the carriage to fetch us," said she, decisively. "Tell Jean to wait for us at the corner of the road by the Captain's new shed."

"Ah, yes, the machine is not working at this

hour," said Fontaine, "or else it is hardly the place where I would recommend a carriage to wait."

It was settled. Fournier marched off to his evening paper; we started in couples and triples across the fields. I was surprised to notice Madame Valmy's childish excitement. She was nodding and wriggling in a sort of exaggeration of her usual ways. Pauline plodded alongside. Monsieur Fontaine had offered his arm to Madame Fournier, who had tied her handkerchief under her chin.

Allow me to compliment you upon this extremely becoming toilette," I heard the Maire saying to her. "Sprigs upon a white ground are always in good taste."

Captain Thompson was still ruminating upon the accident. "Spilt milk. There's a proverb about spilt milk. It was a mercy her arm wasn't burnt, she would not have been able to come this evening. I don't know if you young ladies mean to dance. I think I would take a turn myself if I could find any one to take pity on me. You may well look surprised, Miss Mary. But I don't know how it is," said the little man, "everything seems so happy, and though I'm a middle-aged man, yet I feel as if I were a boy again. I have been very fortunate, I have had better luck than I deserve all my life, and now this sweet angel has taken pity on me and consents to take me under her wing. No wonder I feel young."

CHAPTER VIII.

A COUNTRY DANCE.

A PEASANTS' dance is always a pretty, half-merry, half melancholy festivity to persons looking on. The open air, the rustle of trees, the mingled daylight and darkness, the freshness, the roughness, the odd jingling of the country music, the rustic rhythm of the dancers; the country people coming across fields and skirting the high-roads; some feeling of the long years of hard work before them, of their daily toil intermitted; the echoes sounding across the darkening landscape—all these things touch one with some strange feeling of sympathy and compassion for the merrymakers. We were bound to a certain open green at Étournelles where the villagers used to meet and dance on Sundays after church, while the elders looked on, smoked their pipes, and made their comments to the merry jigging and jingling of their children's pleasures. The refreshments were simple enough, and consisted of a little beer, a few cakes, or pears, baked in the country ovens, and set upon a wooden board under a tree. The music was made by a boy blowing on a pipe, an old man scraping a fiddle, sometimes on grand occasions such as this a second fiddle was forthcoming, with an occasional chorus of voices from the people dancing. When the grand ladies and gentlemen from the houses all round about came to look on, the voices would be shy and hushed for a time. But soon the restraint would wear off; the dancers, carried away by the motion and the exhilaration of all this bouncing and swinging, would burst out anew; sometimes the fine people themselves would be seized with some sudden fancy to foot it with the rest. The grand gentlemen would ask the village maidens to dance, or lead forward one of their own blushing ladies, half shy, half bold.

Pauline was shy to-night, and when Maurice invited her, as he was in duty bound to do, she hung back a little ashamed, and yet, as I could see, she was only wanting a few words from him to give her courage. Her eyes looked so kind, her smile was so humble and yet so sweet for an instant. She blushed. "Won't you come?" said he gaily.

"Don't you see that the child is timid," said Madame Valmy, hastily. "I will begin! I am an old woman, I have faced more terrible things than a village dance. Will you hold my fan, M. Fontaine, and my shawl?"

Maurice could only offer his arm with ready alacrity.

Fontaine bowed and took the fan. Pauline's happy eyes seem to grow dim. The country people looked on, they had whispered a little to each other, hung back for a few minutes, and then again they seemed to be caught up by the wave, and to forget our presence. The tree rustled over our heads, and some birds awakened by the music chirped a note or two. The fields lay darkling round us, a great round pale moon slowly ascended from beyond the distant willow-trees. Its faint rays lit up the dark fields beyond, and the canal gleamed; so did the tiled roof of the new machine-house as it glittered in the light of this cold river of light.

Madame Fournier found a seat on a bench under a tree, Pauline and I stood beside her; our gentlemen came and went. There was a paper lantern hanging from a branch just over Madame Fournier's head, so that she seemed a sort of beacon to return to at intervals. Captain Thompson, seeing that Sidonie was dancing, invited me. We did not join the general circle, but chose a modest corner in the shade, where he and

I danced a little polka to the music on our own account.

When he brought me back to Madame Fournier, Madame Valmy with a lively sign of the head was just going off a second time with M. le Comte.

"Ah! Capitaine," said Fontaine, who was standing by, "we are admiring Madame Valmy's graceful talent. Yes, from out yonder you will see them better." "Admirable man!" said the Maire, looking after him. "There he goes! Times are changed since I first knew Madame Valmy. Look at her, what grace, what gaiety. Ah! here is our good doctor. How do you do, Jobard? What are you doing here?"

"I have been to see Madelon at the mill," said Jobard, with a professional air. "She sleeps, eats, the symptoms are good; I feared cholera, but there is no danger whatever. I am glad to see Madame Valmy enjoying herself so much. She too has been indisposed. She sent for me only yesterday; my medicine has done her good. How she goes round! Look at her! round and round!"

"Madame Valmy indisposed!" said Fontaine; "she never complained to me!"

"Oh!" said Jobard (he was a little, high-

shouldered, shuffling man), "it has been a mere nothing—malaise! migraine! want of sleep, want of
sleep! She could not close her eyes for the rats
in that garret. I know them. I lived in the house
that winter after poor M. Valmy died. There was
noise enough to wake a regiment, wind in the
chimney, rats and mice racing in the wainscot, and
that tree outside creaking and swaying. Along with
Madame Valmy's medicine, I sent some physic for
messieurs the rats, which I found very efficacious
when I was there. Those old houses, they are all
alike. I infinitely prefer my present domicile." And
Jobard, seeing a patient, walked on with a bow to
Madame Fournier.

"Excellent man!" said Fontaine aloud, as Jobard walked off through the crowd, then he continued, lowering his voice: "He may well complain
of the noises in that house; there are those who
assure me that rats can hardly account for the
extraordinary noises which are heard in the Pavilion
at times. Those who believe in the supernatural
declare that—but we will not talk of it. La Mère
Coqueau, you know her—her daughter married
Leroux, the blacksmith—once ventured to ask
Mademoiselle Julienne her impression. She says
she shall never forget the look in the woman's
face."

"Madame Coqueau is an old gossip," said Pauline impatiently. "Why are you always quoting her, M. Fontaine?"

"She has played her rôle," said Fontaine, slightly offended. "I do not wish to bring her again upon the scene." Pauline, however, was not listening to the Maire, but to the music, and her eyes were following Maurice and Madame Valmy twirling in time to it. The two fiddles were answering each other with some fresh sudden spirit, and the whole company seemed stamping in time to the measure. A little wind came blowing from across the fields.

Madame Fournier, who liked anything in the shape of a medical disquisition, now began asking with some interest how M. Valmy died. "It was an unhealthy season," said Fontaine with his eloquent finger. "He had caught some chill out in his peat-fields, and he sent for Dr. Jobard. He seemed recovering, they talked of moving to Paris next day, when in the evening he was suddenly attacked with stomach cramp. Jobard was again sent for—I fetched him myself. He did everything that could be done, applied cataplasms of bran, prescribed infusions of tea, and of violets. I called to inquire the first thing in the morning. Madame Valmy was most unremitting in her attentions; she allowed

no one else to come near him, gave him every
medicine, watched him night and day; nothing
was neglected; it was all in vain; he died, poor
man, and so much the better for everybody. You
would not recognise Madame Valmy now if you
had seen her then. Have you ever remarked
a blue scar upon her throat?" said Fontaine,
in a whisper, for Maurice and his partner were
dancing past us at that moment. "Shall I tell
you—"

"I have no curiosity for such details," interrupted Pauline coldly. "She has evidently forgotten
her troubles, whatever they may have been."

"But this cholera is alarming," said Madame
Fournier, with placid persistence.

"A man and an old woman died at Etournelles
last year," said Fontaine, "and you know what terrible mortality we have had in Paris."

"So it *was* cholera," said Pauline.

"Dr. Jobard had no doubt whatever on the subject," replied the Maire.

"I never pay the slightest attention to anything
that Dr. Jobard says," cried Pauline.

"Pardon me, Mademoiselle" (in a reproving tone).
"Our excellent doctor has had great experience both

with cattle and human subjects. He described the theory of cholera to me only the other day; it is proved to be some subtle poison which penetrates the system. Valmy, predisposed to absorb the miasma, fell a victim to its fatal influence. . . . . Mademoiselle," said the Maire, interrupting himself suddenly, "they are playing a country dance; will you not honour me?" The fiddlers had changed their key.

Madame Valmy came gaily up, sliding her feet, leaning back on her partner's arm. She looked into Pauline's face with her sparkling blue eyes. "Dear Pauline," she said, "you must spare M. Maurice to me for this one more dance; I am positively a child where dancing is concerned. I could go on for hours."

It certainly occurred to me that Pauline and I were a great deal younger than she was, and not less inclined to dance. Pauline, however, refused Fontaine's invitation, although I heard Madame Fournier nervously urging her to take a turn. The girl was very pale, very determined. She wished to remain by her mother, she said.

It was at her suggestion that Fontaine offered me his arm, and we set off together, but Pauline's looks haunted me, and I thought that my partner also was pre-occupied.

Sometimes as we twirled in time, and advanced and retreated, I caught sight of Captain Thompson's little round face, anxiously watching his beautiful Sidonie in her flights.

"She dances too much," said Fontaine, who was also on the look-out. "When people have had such a life as hers, they are apt to forget everything when pleasure comes in their way. But I can see that Thompson, who is the best fellow in the world, is vexed. Valmy never allowed her to dance. Perhaps he was in the right."

Fontaine seemed haunted by some spirit of reminiscence that evening. At every pause in the dance he kept returning to the story he had been telling us. "Who would believe in the past, who saw her now?" he said. "I know for certain she was once met flying from her home, but Valmy came after her, and she went back to him. They say he kept her locked up for three months on that occasion. It was then he had the gate leading from the courtyard to the garden fastened up."

There was something revolting to me in the thought of a woman, who had suffered so much, now apparently forgetting it all to the sound of a fiddle; forgetting her own past, and another person's present—so it seemed to me. She appeared to have no scruples; she absorbed Maurice that evening, without a thought for Pauline, or for Captain Thompson, who went away, I think, for I saw him no more. Maurice asked Pauline to dance once again, but it was evident that it was only from a sense of duty that he did so; and if Pauline consented, it was only to give a countenance to Maurice himself, and to prevent people from saying that he was entirely neglecting his betrothed. It was not a happy evening. Madame Fournier alone should have been satisfied. She made a heroic effort to give her daughter pleasure; her conscience was its own reward.

"Are we never going home, mamma?" said Pauline, wearily.

The music had ceased, the peasants were talking together and buzzing like a swarm of bees. As we were making our way across the green, towards the corner of the road where Madame Fournier had desired her carriage to meet her, we came upon two gentlemen walking arm-in-arm in the shadow. One was Maurice, the other was Fontaine, who seemed to have drawn his companion away from the crowd. It was impossible not to gather portions of the Maire's emphatic sentences as we came along: "You cannot prevent chattering tongues. Your duty to your interesting fiancée—excuse the frankness of an old friend."

Pauline stopped short, shrinking back. "Oh, mamma!" she said, breathing quickly. "Is this true? Everybody talking. Oh, come away. Oh! what shall we do?"

Madame Fournier, with some motherly presence of mind, only shrugged her shoulders. "My dear child, if we listened to all the advice people give, do you think anybody would ever have a moment's peace? Fontaine is a chatterer, who likes to make gossip where it does not exist."

"Ladies, you are going!" cried the Maire, springing forward as he heard his name. "M. le Comte! Mesdames Fournier are going. I will call their carriage," he continued, talking on to hide his embarrassment.

The music had begun again. Maurice, looking very black and very stiff, came up to the carriage-door.

"Are you coming with us?" said Madame Fournier, very coldly.

"No, no; remain and dance your dance out," said Pauline, not unkindly, but in a chill, sad voice that seemed to come from a heavy heart. Maurice bowed, and we drove away without him, and reached home in silence.

"Well, have you enjoyed your dance?" said Fournier, when he let us in.

CHAPTER IX.

AN EXPLANATION.

WHEN I saw Madame Fournier again next day, her eyes were red, her face was pale; she looked as if she had not slept, and Fournier himself did not seem to me in much better condition. It was a melancholy morning. The old couple kept together. Fournier avoided De Mesnil; Madame Fournier treated him with ceremonious politeness. Pauline, I think, must have guessed what was coming; she stayed in her room all the morning, and sat over her embroidery, stitching and stitching as women do who are anxious, and who cannot trust themselves to cease from work. De Mesnil did not appear at luncheon.

M. Fournier had pulled his little black velvet skullcap over his eyes, he had tucked his afternoon newspaper, unopened, under his arm; he was walking up and down the hall, crossing and recrossing the great square of light by the open door; his coffee was standing on a table, cooling and untasted; his brows were bent, his steps were hurried and heavy.

Fontaine's remarks, as repeated by Madame Fournier, had made a great impression upon him. It was all the more vivid because the Maire had seemed to him to speak his own impressions. It does not matter whether impressions are real or imaginary, the fact of another person unexpectedly speaking out what we have secretly felt seems to give a sudden life to our silence. The feeling becomes a part of real things, it gains speech and action; it is life itself, and ceases to be a criticism. Fournier's idea that Maurice was trifling with his daughter, and not behaving well by her, now seemed to take consistency and shape, voice and action; all his deep tenderness for Pauline turned to indignation against Maurice. But I don't imagine that Fournier, good father as he was, quite understood what it was he was asking of his daughter when he expected her to give up suddenly and immediately the wonderful, new, irresistible interest which had come into her existence. All her life Pauline had wanted affection, and though she had known Maurice only for a few weeks, the instinct to love and to devote herself had been there long before. She had been told that he was the person with whom the rest of her life was to be spent, she had felt that it was to him that her heart went out unhesitatingly; it seemed so natural to love him, so unnatural not to love him. Her affection for him seemed to her something quite independent of his affection for her—in the same way as a mother's affection for her child does not depend upon that child's feeling for her. When her father called, Pauline came hurrying up to ask what he wanted. What was it he was saying as he marched up and down? He told her that he could allow this trifling no longer, that she must take courage and face the truth, and acknowledge it to herself; that De Mesnil was playing with her, acting dishonourably; it was as if some one had suddenly struck a heavy blow upon her heart.

"What do you mean, papa?" said Pauline, leaning back against the billiard-table. "Why do you say this?" she asked, speaking with dry, parched lips. She had known what was coming, but she had put it away all that day.

The old man was so unhappy at what he had to say that he answered sharply, from pain of the pain he was giving.

"You know what it means as well as I do, Pauline," he said. "I am not a patient man; I cannot wait in silence, and see my daughter insulted, while I, her father, am outraged, defied. Look; can you not see for yourself? Have you no dignity, my child?"

"I hope not," says Pauline. 'What has dignity got to do with what one feels in one's heart? Dignity is for outside things."

"Hush, Pauline; don't talk such nonsense!" cried Fournier, exasperated; and indeed I could understand it.

By some unlucky chance, at this very minute our usual visitors came along the terrace, the Captain and the Maire and Madame Valmy, and Maurice, who had been walking up and down an hour past and who had seen them coming, and gone to meet them. The Captain was a little ahead, talking to Fontaine. The two gentlemen did not enter the house at once, but turned up the path that leads to the stables.

Maurice had stopped short, unconscious of the eyes that were fixed upon them. He was gazing up into Sidonie's face. She was half turning away, half accepting his homage.

"To-morrow," cries Fournier, furious, "he goes back to his garret! That devil of a woman may follow him if she chooses. My daughter and I wash our hands of him. Such conduct is not to be entertained by honest people. Do you hear, Pauline?"

"I hear you, papa," says Pauline. "It is enough to break my marriage, without breaking my ears as well;" and then she changed; somehow a great blush came into her face, and she said, "One thing I ask, which is, that you do not condemn Maurice unheard. I shall never care for any one else; never, papa, never; remember that. I shall not forget, even though he may forget me."

"Is this the way you speak? you, a modest girl brought up at your mother's side," cries Fournier, furious, bothered, and affected.

"Well, then, I am not modest," cries Pauline. "And the thing that I am most grateful to you for is that you have brought me up to think for myself. I am not like Marie des Ormes in her blue and white. I am not a gentle, obedient, young girl. I respect my parents; I will not act against their wishes. But, oh! that it should be you, of all the people in the world, to make me so unhappy," cried Pauline, with a great burst of tears, throwing herself into her father's arms. "And, oh! I love him, father, with all my heart I love Maurice."

"My child," cried poor Fournier, "it is not I who make you unhappy. Don't, my dear one, I beseech you, do not cry. It is that imbecile out yonder. Look at him, he has forgotten your very existence. May the devil take that woman! The day will come when you will thank your old father."

"Let Maurice come and explain for himself,"

cried Pauline, very loud and not caring who heard
her. "Maurice! Maurice!" she called, going to the
door. Maurice heard Pauline's voice calling across
the terrace. I saw him turn, say something hastily
to his companion, and come hurrying towards the
house. His face looked so pale and scared, his eyes
so bright and wild, that it seemed to me that he was
at least no heartless, indifferent actor in the play that
was being played out.

Pauline was still standing at the door when
Maurice came up. She went up to him and put out
her hand, but he did not take it. She began at
once without any preamble.

"I called you; I want to hear the truth from
yourself. Do you know what my father is telling
me?" she said. "He says that all that has passed between us must come to an end; that you must go back
to Paris, and that I must stay here and marry somebody else. What do you say to his plan? What do
you say to it?" she repeated shrilly, with her eyes
fixed upon his face.

For a minute Maurice was silent.

"What does he say? Who cares what he says?"
cried Monsieur Fournier, almost brutally. "All he
has got to do now is to hold his tongue. I don't
suppose he wishes for any explanations from me. If

he does, he may chance to hear things which may not please him."

"You cannot tell me anything I do not already know, that I have not already told myself," said the young man, speaking in a low, thrilling voice, quickly and distinctly. "You may say to me anything you please, it is only what I deserve to hear. The deep respect and gratitude I feel for all your daughter's goodness and——"

"Be silent!" shouts Fournier, in a rage. "Do you suppose that any one here wants your fine speeches? Take them where they are in request, but do not insult my daughter by such professions after your conduct."

"He does not insult me, papa," Pauline said; "I believe him." There was something touching in the girl's honest accent. "I believe him and so do you," and she took her father's hand in both hers as she spoke—"I am not going to marry him. I could not if it is true that he feels as you think. I do not wonder at it." Her voice faltered. "But you see I can understand it all, and I daresay I should do the same as he, and be ready to leave the people who cared the most for me for those I felt I loved the best."

Her steady voice failed; she could scarcely finish her sentence, and she turned from us and ran quickly upstairs to her room, passing Madame Fournier, who was leisurely creaking down from her afternoon nap to wakeful life again. Madame Valmy also appeared at the same instant smiling in the doorway. I wondered she had the courage to walk up as usual. With an impatient exclamation Fournier moved away.

"This is intolerable. Come in here. I have to speak to you in private," he said to the Comte. And he walked to his study followed by the young man.

"What is it, mon ami?" asked Madame Fournier, trotting in after them.

"What is happening?" says Madame Valmy, looking round. "Why has everybody run away?" and she settled her laces and gently flirted her fan. "Here you are; have you been to the stables?" she said, as the Captain and Fontaine now joined us. "All the Fournier family are shut up in there," said she, pointing.

"They seem engaged on some very mysterious business," says Madame Valmy, sinking back for a moment in a big chair.

We could hear voices rising and falling behind the closed door, and more than one angry burst from Fournier. I think Madame Valmy might have guessed what it was all about had she tried to do so.

"I am privileged, I will ascertain," said Fontaine, walking with precaution across the hall and knocking carefully at the door.

"Who is there?" shouts Fournier from within.

Fontaine opens the panel a little way, slides in —the door is again shut. Madame Valmy shrugs her shoulders and begins to walk about the room.

"That is a pretty print," says she, looking at a framed plan of Sebastopol which was hanging on the wall. Then with a slight yawn, "I am tired," she said. "I think I should like to go home, if Mademoiselle Mary will make my excuses to Madame Fournier when the mysterious business is over. Take me home, Beauvoir."

Captain Thompson started up delighted. It was not often that his lovely intended would consent to come away under his exclusive escort.

"Yes, you are tired; you should rest," he said. "Yes, let us go at once. You are not strong, Sidonie; you never spare yourself." In this he was quite mistaken, poor man; but if Sidonie had wished to spare herself a scene she was too late, for at this moment Pauline, still looking very pale, but quite composed, came down the stairs again, and as Madame Valmy was going, she called to her to stop.

"Is Maurice already gone down to the village?" Pauline asked.

"Are you going?"

"Why do you ask *me?*" said Madame Valmy. "He is still here, I believe; but I am not his keeper. It is not me he is obliged to marry;" and she turned with a curious feminine dart, and took Captain Thompson's arm.

"Come, Beauvoir," she said; "Mademoiselle Fournier will be best without us."

"No, I want to speak to you," said Pauline, gravely; "stay for a minute."

"I will go outside!" cried Captain Thompson, still quite unconscious. "I will smoke my cigar, and when you young ladies have had your confab, call me back, Sid, for you ought to get home."

He walked away. Madame Valmy was, I think, curious to know what Pauline had to say. She let him go, after a moment's hesitation, and came to meet the girl with an odd smile.

"Have you had a quarrel?" she asked; "do you want me to help you to make it up? I'm afraid it *was* very naughty of him to dance with me all last night; but I have got him into good training for you, and you ought to be grateful," she said, with a laugh.

Sidonie was not used to simple outspoken natures such as Pauline, and she did not calculate upon the consequences of her ill-timed joke.

"Listen," said Pauline, in her dogmatic way; "do not think that I do not blame you because I am silent? Why did you come in our way? I could have made him happy, I think, if it had not been for you. You say you are not going to marry him. Do you think it is any comfort to me that he is to be made unhappy too? Are you acting honestly by us all?"

As Pauline spoke, a sort of light came into her eyes and a tone into her voice. She looked far handsomer at that moment than Madame Valmy, as she stood her ground, sincere, indignant, alive, uttering her protest against wrong.

Madame Valmy seemed to me to grow pale, then grey; all the beautiful colour died out of her cheeks, all the glitter out of her hair; she laughed a nasty little shrill whistling laugh. "What a dear impetuous child you are," she said, "and what foolish, foolish things you take into your silly little head! What have I to do with all this? M. de Mesnil comes to see me. I gave him a lesson in dancing last night. I have a great regard for him, and am only too glad to make him welcome; but, my dear child, do you imagine for one instant that I wish to interfere with your claims upon his attention? You should be more careful before you make such unfounded assertions;" and Madame Valmy drew herself up; she had found her part, so it seemed to me. At first, taken by surprise, she had really not known what to say or what attitude to take. It was one thing to be secretly enjoying Pauline's mortification and her own sense of power and Maurice's unconcealed devotion, and another to be called to account by her outspoken rival; questioned, rebuked, and desired to marry him on the spot. This seemed the strangest complication of all, and I could quite understand Madame Valmy's objections to pledge herself to any definite course.

"Do you mean that, notwithstanding all that has passed, you are not sure of your feelings?" said Pauline.

At this moment the hall-door opened, and Thompson's head was put in. "Nearly ready?" said he.

"Of this I feel sure, that Captain Thompson will protect me, and that you have strangely forgotten yourself, Pauline, in the way in which you have been speaking!" cried Madame Valmy, greatly relieved by the interruption. "Tell her, Beauvoir," she said, twirling swiftly round, "that you will not see me insulted by cruel suspicion," and, as chance would have it, as she pointed to Pauline, with a sob, the study-door opened, and Maurice, of the pale face, came out. The wretched woman now turned towards him, still holding by Captain Thompson's arm. "M. Maurice,"

she said, "I will not, cannot believe that you are
aware of the things which have been said to me.
Oh, it is too dreadful!" and she buried her face in
her hands for an instant.

Poor Maurice looked from one to the other. He
had himself only just escaped from an agitating
scene, in which Mr. Fournier had certainly not
spared Madame Valmy; and for a moment it seemed
to him as if all the blame at which he had been
chafing had been poured out upon her head. She
looked at him with such appealing eyes, she was so
pale, so trembling. Thompson was stepping forward,
also prepared to do battle for his Sidonie, but not
quite knowing whom to attack, nor what to complain
of. Pauline stood defiant, with flashes of sullen dis-
pleasure. She blushed crimson when Maurice looked
at her reproachfully. It seemed to him at the time
that her looks accused her, poor child.

"I need scarcely tell you that I am not account-
able for what may have been said to pain you," he
said, in a low, indignant voice. "I can only beg
you, madame, who are generous, to forgive those
who may have been wanting in generosity."

"Forgive, forgive," said the Captain; "that is not
the question. Of course, one forgives real injuries;
but people should be careful before giving way to
their silly tempers, and remember that they give a

great deal of unnecessary pain and annoyance. I am sure Mademoiselle Fournier will be the first to regret this to-morrow morning. Come along, Sid, it is time we got home."

He pulled Madame Valmy's arm through his, and the two walked away together. Maurice was already gone; poor Pauline stood silent, self-reproach-ful, overwhelmed; it suddenly seemed to her that she had been ridiculous, unkind, unreasonable; she turned pale, hard, stupid; she stood in the centre of the hall; all the fire was gone out of her eyes.

Was it so, had she been ungenerous? Maurice said so, and his look of reproach had pierced her more than his words.

We were all silent in the study that evening; the green lamp was trimmed; books and newspapers lay upon the table, the servants had lighted a wood fire, which was comfortably crackling. Pauline added some logs, and sat down on a low stool be-fore the flame, resting her chin against her hands. Madame Fournier watched her with an anxious face for a time, then settled herself for a nap in the big arm-chair. Fontaine, who had remained at Four-nier's request, sat down to a game of écarté by the light of the green lamp. There was something homely and tranquil in this interior: the peaceful crackling of the fire, the even glow of the lamp, the' quiet slumbers of the old woman in her chimney-corner—all diffused a certain sense of peace and of repose, only all the room seemed to me somehow full of the pain in poor Pauline's sad and aching eyes.

The window was uncurtained. The clouds were drifting across the sky, and the moon was on the wane. Once I thought I heard a cry coming faintly from a long way off. Fontaine put down his cards for an instant.

"It is only some bird or animal," said he.

Pauline started from her dream, and presently went to the window and looked out for a minute, and soon after left the room. She did not come back any more that night. For the first time in her young life, she had been met and overwhelmed by one of those invisible currents of feeling which carry people, and boundaries, and stationary things all before them, until little by little the stormy stream subsides. Pauline, who had been so confident, so intolerant for others, was strangely humbled and overcome by the force of her own emotions. She had despised people who "gave way." What was this strange new power that had laid its relentless hand upon her? She hated herself, but all the same she could not help the suspicions, the self-reproaches, the emotions, which distracted her so cruelly. When generous and well-meaning people suspect others of wrong, it is an almost intolerable pain and humiliation. The thought recurs, it cannot be put away, but it spoils all peace of mind, all tranquil enjoyment of life. Mistrust of oneself is perhaps the worst form of this phase of feeling, and Pauline had suddenly lost confidence in her own infallibility.

CHAPTER X.

THE LODGE IN THE GARDEN OF CUCUMBERS.

When I awoke next morning, she was standing by my bedside. She looked pale and haggard. She had not been able to sleep all night, she told me.

"I want you to do something for me," she said. "I want you to dress quickly and to come with me to the village. Madame Valny is going. I know it —never mind how I know it. I think my mind would be more at ease if I could see her once more. Perhaps I was hard upon her yesterday. Am I jealous? Is that what ails me?" She pushed back the curtain from the window and threw it open. All the sweet autumnal light came floating in from the garden without, and a golden withered leaf from the creeper overhanging the balcony dropped on to the wooden floor. The fragrant breath of morning seemed to fill the room. For a minute Pauline stood leaning against the window rail, looking out across the park and the fields beyond, towards the thatched village with its belfry and enclosing poplar-trees. Then she turned, smiling with a sweet look in her face, something like the autumnal sunshine, at once troubled and sincere. She signed to me to lose no time, and left the room.

The house was scarcely awake when we left it, hurrying down by the little side-path leading to the canal. I remember the look of that early morning so well! The delicate fragrant perfume from the burnt leaves, the stir in the foliage, through which the stems were beginning to show, the tranquil faint tones of the sky, and the wheeling flight of a great company of birds high overhead. At the turn of the road we met the postman, in his blue linen smock, with dusty boots. He had a letter for me, he said, and one for M. Fournier, which sent a sudden glow into Pauline's pale cheek, for she recognised M. de Mesnil's writing. I opened my letter as I walked along. It was heavily weighted, and contained the long-missing key for which I had written, and a letter in verse from my kind old uncle, who sometimes amused himself by this style of composition: "Pocket and lock it," "easy and Visy," and so on. I would have read it to Pauline, but she would not listen, and only hurried faster and faster along the road. She would not tell me at first how it was that she knew of Madame Valmy's plans, but after a while she suddenly said, "I do not know why I do not tell you at once.

Maurice came up last night. I saw him coming when I was at the window, and I went to meet him, and he told me of this. He told me other things," she said with a strange sort of burst. "It all seems so miserable, so strange! Will you be silent if I trust you? He adores her. She has promised to marry him in a year. Why did he tell me? Why did he tell me?"

"Why, indeed!" said I. "Pauline, he is a miserable creature." But Pauline would not let me blame him.

"It was to exonerate her, he told me," she said. "He asked me to think more kindly of her. And now," said Pauline, "I do not know whether or not I think more kindly of her."

"But is she not going to tell the Captain?" I asked. "Is she going on deceiving him? Are you not going to tell him, Pauline?"

"I!" cried the girl, with a sort of laugh. "Do you think it my place? The worst part is to come," she said, in a dry, matter-of-fact voice. "Madame Valmy has assured Maurice that the Captain is ill— that he has not a year to live, and that is why she keeps silence. It might kill him, she says, to know the truth. For my part, I had rather die of a truth than live upon a lie, I think. But Madame Valmy likes to arrange her life to her circumstances," and Pauline broke off; a burning blush came over her face.

"I think you should speak to your father," I said.

"I want to see her first," said Pauline, now quite piteous. "She might say something to undo all this horrible doubt. Maurice believes in her. For his sake I try and believe in her too."

When we came to the Pavilion the great gates were open; the chickens were pecking in the court-yard; there seemed to be not a soul about the place.

"They went at seven o'clock, driving with the luggage. Madame Coqueau is to come and keep the house," said little Jeanne Picard, who was peep-ing in at the gate. "She has not yet arrived; she is gone to see to the cows."

Pauline did not answer. She stood still for an instant — then she walked in, crossed the yard, mounted the stone steps, and marched straight into the drawing-room, where all the chairs and tables were pushed about just as they had been left the night before. The newspaper lay on the floor; one of the Captain's gloves had been forgotten in a chair; the shutters were half-closed, the daylight came freshly shining in and reflected from the flower-glasses and the pretty ornaments all about the room. On a sofa a little piece of work was lying. It was a cigar-case, of embroidered canvas, with an elaborate M interwoven with coronets. Pauline took it up, looked at it for an instant, flung it down once more, and then suddenly dropping into the corner of the sofa, hid her face away, and I could see that she was crying. I was obliged to rouse her almost immediately, for I heard some one coming. As usual it was Fontaine. He had seen us pass by, and now entered the room with an exclamation— fresh from his morning toilet.

Pauline made an effort, choked down her tears, and met him quietly. As I think of it all it seems like a vague sort of dream; so disjointed, so sudden and tragical were the events which followed.

"You are too late," said the Maire, cheerfully. "Our good friends are gone! They have stolen a march upon us. The Captain drove Madame Valmy to the station early this morning; they were to take the train at Etournelles: he told me he wanted to leave some directions with his manager there. His man was to take the luggage to Corbeil and rejoin them there. Mademoiselle Julienne was not with her mistress. I don't know how she went," said Fontaine, thoughtfully. "Possibly she started last night. I don't know what called the Captain away. I think he was anxious, and wished to consult a physician."

"For his health?" said Pauline, quickly.

"For her health," said Fontaine. "He told me himself that she was strange — hysterical; that he was not easy, and did not trust Jobard entirely," said the Maire, lightly.

"Madame Valmy not well!" said Pauline, vehemently. "Monsieur Fontaine, is it only Madame Valmy you have been anxious about? Tell me, do you believe what she tells people in confidence, that he is suffering from a mortal disease?"

She had spoken at last, and Monsieur Fontaine seemed taken aback.

"A mortal disease," he repeated. "Pray explain yourself, Mademoiselle. I really cannot follow you."

"How can I explain myself?" cried Pauline, all excited. "Is it my business? Am I a spy set to watch other people? I am a wicked, suspicious girl, Monsieur Fontaine. I came here to confess to her, but she is gone, and I don't know—I don't know what I mean." And she burst out crying once more and hid her face in her hands.

"My dear lady, you are ill—out of sorts. No wonder, after all that has occurred. Come away, come home with me. Let us consult Jobard; that good fellow will give you some soothing mixture," cried the Maire, very kind, full of concern. "What is it? do not be alarmed. Yes. I too hear something. What can it be?" said he, seeing me looking about. "Wait here—pray wait here; I will return," he cried, divided between his concern for Pauline and his intelligent interest in everything going on.

What was it? I had heard it for some time. It seemed a dull muffled knocking, and now and then, so I thought, came the echo of a human voice calling out, so faintly that one might well mistake it. "It is not in the village," I said.

"It is something in the house," said Pauline, decidedly, listening with all her might.

"Can it be the little Picards at their play?" said the Maire, doubtfully.

"No. I think it is in the garret," said Mademoiselle Fournier, suddenly hurrying out of the room. The Pavilion, as indeed all the houses in the village, had empty garrets under the roof where people hung their clothes to dry, and kept their lumber and their apples from one year's end to another. I followed her as she ran up the wooden staircase and climbed the flight which led to the topmost garret, of which she threw the door wide open.

All was silent here. The place was empty. The light was streaming in through the sashless windows; a few white clothes were still hanging upon a line; the rats and mice were safe in their holes.

"There is nothing here," said Pauline. "Come down—it must be from below."

Fontaine was standing, looking very pale, at the foot of the stairs as we came down.

"The sound comes from the cellar out of the dining-room," said he. "There is something shut up in there."

I knew the ways of the house—having lived there—better than they did, and I could now tell them which was the way.

"This is the door which leads to the outer cellar," said I. "Here is a key that fits it," and I pulled mine out from my pocket.

"Effectively there is no key in the door," said Fontaine. "How do you come by this one?"

16*

"It is not wanted, the door is only bolted," said Pauline, who had taken the key from my hand, and drawn back the massive iron bolt as she spoke. When she opened the heavy door a damp breath of vault-like atmosphere seemed to meet us. The knocking became louder and more distinct; and the voice —shall I ever forget the strange terror of that despairing voice?—seemed to be coming out of the darkness, and calling and calling.

"Take care; there are steps within," I whispered, too frightened to speak out.

Pauline, however, walked in unhesitatingly. She swept against some bottle, and it fell with a crash upon the ground. Suddenly the knocking ceased— it seemed as if the person within was listening too. Fontaine, who had left us, came back with a light almost immediately, and then we could see the dark damp vault and the flight of steps before us. I had often fetched the wine out of this outer cellar, and peeped down the black flight which led to the inner vault, where Madame Valmy kept her best cider, so I had been told. Now as the light flashed I saw it all in its usual order. There were the bottles; the one Pauline knocked over Fontaine picked up and put back in its place. There stood the two chests that we had put away; there was the dark flight leading to the mildewy door of the lower cellar. It was fast closed with bars and rusty-headed nails.

"Open, open, open, madame!" screamed the voice; and somehow in one moment we all recognised it as that of Julienne. "If you do not open I will knock the house down and denounce you. Open, open—I know you are there; I hear your silk dress on the stones. Speak—why don't you speak?—for pity speak. Have you spared him? Mercy for us both—mercy, mercy. Valmy was a monster, but this one is a good man. Spare him—spare me. Have I ever said one word? I will be silent. Only spare me. Oh, Madame, I entreat you, have pity."

"Julienne, is it you?" said Pauline, falteringly. But Fontaine signed to her to be silent, and put his hand on his mouth.

"What do you say?" cried the voice; and the hands within began to thump and bang again. "If you do not let me out I will live, I will escape to denounce you. Let me out—let me out."

"I am not Madame Valmy; I am Pauline Fournier," said Pauline, speaking very loud. "Do not be afraid, Julienne. We will open the door and let you out."

There came a half-suppressed scream of horror from within—then silence.

"Perhaps our outer key would fit this door too," said I.

"No," said Pauline, "I have tried it. It will not go in."

"This is horrible. We must get the locksmith at once," said Fontaine. "Will you ladies wait here and tranquillise the poor thing if you can? She is half out of her mind."

"Yes," said Pauline. And then, as soon as he was gone, still calling through the door, she tried to reassure the wild creature within.

"Is it you, Mademoiselle? Don't leave me—don't leave me!" shrieked Julienne once more. "I am mad—quite mad! Oh, do not heed what I say." Then suddenly she seemed to remember herself. "Oh, what have I done? Leave me. Lose no time —follow them—warn her. Tell her you know all. And oh, for pity, Mademoiselle, spare us—do not betray her. Oh, for pity's sake do not betray her."

I own that I was trembling in every limb—the time seemed endless.

"M. Fontaine is a long time," said Pauline. "Should you mind going to see if any one is coming. Oh, please do go," she said, "go to Leroux and tell him to come at once and open the door for us. There is no time to lose."

"Shan't you be frightened," I said, "here alone?"

"No," said Pauline, impatiently. "Only go, please go."

My strength seemed to return with the fresh air. It seemed strange to come out alive, and breathing and unhurt, into the commonplace street. I had not far to go. The locksmith lived at the end of the village, by the church. As I hurried along I met the Curé, who looked at me and seemed about to speak, but I passed him quickly. Even then I noticed a little group in a doorway. It seemed to me that they also looked up, broke off, and then began to speak again. I was too much excited and preoccupied to pay much attention to stray looks and words, but in my horrible agitation and excitement it already seemed to me that our secret had spread, and that people were suspecting and discussing the truth in hurried whispers. Had Fontaine been wasting time making confidences all along the road? I did him injustice. The locksmith's door was closed, and for some minutes I knocked and thumped in vain. At last I heard slow steps, and when the door was opened, Leroux's aged mother appeared on the threshold, with a child in her arms.

"Be quiet," said she. "My daughter-in-law is ill. What do you want?"

"I want your son," said I, breathless. "M. Fontaine wants him at once—it is of importance that he should come at once."

"He can't come," said the old woman, shaking her head. "He was fetched—have not you heard of what has happened? There has been an accident to a carriage." Here the child began to cry, and its grandmother to hush it on her shoulder. "Eh! yes; an accident," said the old woman, slowly. "The Captain's horse took fright down by the peat-fields. The carriage-wheels are off. My son has gone to see if he can fix them on again, to bring back the unfortunate wounded."

"The wounded!—who is wounded?" I asked, all dazed.

"No one knows for certain," said the old woman, still hushing the wailing child. "Some say it is the lady, some say it is the Captain who is killed."

Then a voice called from within. She went back, still hushing the child, and abruptly closed the door. It was all very miserable. I turned very faint. I felt it a great relief at that minute to see Fournier turning the corner by the church. Fontaine was with him. The two were walking rapidly, and Fontaine was carrying some tools in his hands. I ran to meet them. They were speaking excitedly. Fournier quickly broke off to ask me why I had left Pauline alone.

"She sent me," said I. "The time seemed so long. Do not wait for me now. Please go to her."

"You had better wait outside and rest," said Fournier. "Poor child! all this has been too much for you."

"And there is more to come," cried Fontaine. "Ah! Mademoiselle, have you heard of this terrible accident? There is hope for the Captain, M. Fournier tells me. It is too much—it is all too terrible!" and he hurried after Fournier, who was walking with his longest strides.

I confess that I could hardly stand; the sunny street, the voices, the horrible events of that morning seemed crowding down upon me in dizzy circles. I think a child came up and said something, but I could not answer. When I reached the Pavilion, I sank down upon the stone steps, for I could not stand, and for a minute I waited to collect my thoughts. As I sat there I could hear the voices inside the house exclaiming, the sound of the crowbar forcing open the lock, and the quiet strokes of the church clock striking nine, followed by the rumble of distant wheels. And then something happened which seemed to me, perhaps, the most strange and unexpected event of all. The kitchen door slowly opened, and Julienne came quietly out in her big black cloak. She had on her usual tidy cap tied under her chin, and a basket on her arm. She looked at me, but did not speak, brushed past me, and walked quickly. I was so startled, I only watched her go across the court. At the gate she met the omnibus just starting for the station at Corbeil. She signed to it to stop, got in, and before I could recover from my surprise, she was gone. Next minute I heard a final crash within, and loud exclamations, and then as I ran in to tell of my strange impression, a dream, a reality, I scarcely knew which, I met Fournier with his daughter clinging to him in tears, followed by the Maire in his shirt-sleeves, in a most extraordinary agitation.

"Was there ever anything so utterly unbelievable! Mademoiselle, could you not have sworn to her voice? There is nothing, absolutely no one in the cellars. Do you understand me? No one— Julienne was not there."

"Julienne passed me a minute ago," I said. "She went across the court. She went off in the diligence to Corbeil." And as I spoke I looked at Pauline, who still stood silent and sobbing by her father's side.

"Oh! Mademoiselle," said Fontaine, turning upon Pauline. "How could you play me this trick? Then it was you who let her out! But are you both demented? You let this witness escape you!" He could not finish for agitation and excitement. Pauline looked imploringly at her father through her tears.

"Well, Paule!" said he, quietly assuming the fact; "speak—why did you let her out, or rather why did you not tell us that you had done so?"

Pauline tried to answer, but she turned pale and very faint for a minute, and could only cling to her father's arm.

The hot sun came pouring down into the little courtyard as we all stood there. The shadows were striking, black and fierce. Pauline waited silent by her father's side, apparently sullen or downcast, and tired out; Fontaine, perfectly bewildered, and still in his shirt-sleeves, stood looking from her to me. The ducks, missing their accustomed meal, came straggling up to be fed, and presently one and another neighbour came in with scared looks and hushed voices. Fournier took his daughter upon his arm and drew her a little aside; he wanted to question her in private, and he also had miserable news to tell; she burst into piteous sobs, and he led her away through the crowd of children and peasant people. I followed with kind Madame Bougie from the grocer's shop, not a little grateful for her friendly exclamations and sympathies. Fournier left us in the shop while he went back to fetch the pony-carriage, for poor Pauline was quite spent and could scarcely stand. Madame Bougie took us into the back parlour with the glass door that opened to the garden. She brought us glasses of orange-flower water, that panacea of French emotions, and her little boy ran in with a nosegay from the garden. She would let in no one else until Fournier's return. Fontaine came to the door, but she drove him off. I was glad of it, for Pauline began to shiver nervously when she heard his voice. I thought it might be a relief to her to speak, and I asked her how it happened that she let Julienne out after I left.

Pauline looked at me hard. "Was it wrong?" said she. Then she started up, and went to the window and looked out; then came back to me. "I tried the key a second time and found it fitted. When you first gave it to me I had turned it wrong. She came out looking all wild," said Pauline. "Oh, she looked so terrible. She had hurt her hands; they were bleeding when she held them up, and she implored me and implored me to let her go.

She told me she had seen Valmy's face in the darkness close beside her, reproaching her for the past; that she knew he would have been still alive if they had cared for him when he was ill; that he died of their neglect. That is what Julienne said, and she had let him die without remorse, and Madame Valmy knew it."

"Oh! how horrible it all is! Oh! what have I done?" cried poor Pauline. She was so agitated I did not like to ask any more questions, it seemed best to leave her to herself.

Pauline was still very much upset when Fournier returned. She told him the whole story, with not a little agitation. He listened without a word.

"Oh, papa," she said, "I will confess to you that I have been half beside myself with such miserable suspicions that I can scarcely bear to think of them. I have not known what to do or how to bear it all. When I heard that Madame Valmy said the poor little Captain must die, some horrible dread came over me which haunted me like an evil spirit; and then when Julienne implored me to let her go, I still believed—I thought if she warned her mistress, it might yet be time to prevent I knew not what evil. Oh, papa, as I think it over, it seems to me like a crime that I have committed. To think a cruel thing is such a hopeless wrong, and now, now it is too late to repent. Oh, what shall I do, what shall I do?"

Poor Pauline was quite overcome by the events of the last few hours which had made clear so much unhappiness. She was trembling in every limb. Fournier did not attempt to comfort her.

"We are all liable to mistake," he said; "all ready to judge our neighbours harshly at times. You and I have, perhaps, been hard upon that poor woman, Pauline, and we must bear our punishment. There is poor Thompson, he has done no wrong, he is dreadfully stricken. It is fortunate that they brought him to your mother to nurse, it was the nearest house."

Then he went on to tell us that the horse had taken fright at the sudden working of the poor Captain's machine, and galloped across the field. Madame Valmy had been thrown against a stone and killed upon the spot; the Captain had fallen under the carriage, and the wheel had passed over him as he lay. It was thought at first that he too was hopelessly hurt, but the accounts were now more reassuring.

How well I remember our drive back to the château through the pretty autumnal avenues, over the bright brown carpet of leaves that had fallen the night before. Pauline was sitting with her head

upon her father's shoulder, quite silent and scared.
I too felt utterly stupefied and bewildered until kind
Madame Fournier met us on the terrace and put
her arms about us. I shall never forget her goodness and motherly tenderness during all the days
that immediately followed the disaster. The poor
Captain lay between life and death; Pauline too,
was ill, and requiring the tenderest care; Madame
Fournier's motherly looks seemed to fall with comfort on one and on another. She undertook to
enlighten Fontaine as to the real events of that
morning.

There is not very much more to tell of these sad
things which happened during my visit to my
friends. Jobard, when cross-questioned by Fournier
and the Maire, solemnly affirmed that the cause of
Valmy's death was cholera. The symptoms were
unmistakable, the patient had rallied, and seemed
recovering, when he suddenly sank from exhaustion.
Jobard himself was present at the time, and had
been administering stimulants. Fournier consulted
with Fontaine and came to the conclusion that there
was no reason to doubt Jobard's professional opinion
deliberately given. One little fact is worth men-
tioning which went far to remove some of our vague
suspicions, and to ease our minds. One day the
Captain began to speak of the events of that fatal

morning, and told Fontaine with a sigh that he believed the accident had turned upon the merest chance. "Just as we were starting," he said, "I went back and saw that the cellar-door had not been closed. . . . Why does one remember such thing? I used to think poor Julienne had a weakness for wine-bottles. "Look there," said he very sadly, holding up his right hand. "I believe that terrible accident came of my turning that key. I sprained my hand against the door, and I was holding the whip and the reins in my left hand when the horse took fright."

One of my cousins was taken ill, and I was sent for home long before the Captain was sufficiently recovered to leave his room. It was perhaps best for him to lie there quietly with the good, kind, worthy Fourniers to keep watch over him, and to prevent the many rumours and suspicions from without from wounding him afresh as he lay upon his bed of sickness.

I have not been to Visy since the day when Pauline kissed me and said farewell by the old gateway; but I can still see her before me, as she was then, when I looked my last at her honest kind face, and at her home with all its friendly doors and windows open to the autumn sunshine. The Captain waved a thin hand from the balcony where they had carried him. Monsieur Fournier was waiting to drive me to the station. I remember the scent of the clematis about the terrace; the sound of the cheerful country servants' voices calling, the glistening of the water as we crossed the little bridge over the canal.

There is one more fact I have to relate concerning my friends at Visy. One day, about a twelve-month later, I received a printed form directed in Captain Thompson's handwriting, which gave me no little surprise. It was the formal announcement by M. and Madame Fournier of the Château of Visy le Roy, and by Miss Marianne and Miss Eliza Thompson of Lancaster, of a marriage contracted according to the Catholic and the Protestant rites, between their daughter Miss Pauline Hermance Louise Mélanie Fournier and their nephew Captain John Beauvoir Thompson, of Amphlett House, near Lancaster.

THE END OF "ACROSS THE PEAT-FIELDS."

MISS MORIER'S VISIONS.

17*

I WAS walking home one evening along an autumnal road, and hurrying, for I was a little be-lated, when I thought I heard a step following mine. I stopped, the step also stopped. I looked back, there was no one to be seen; but when I set off again I once more heard the monotonous footfall. Sometimes it seemed to miss a beat; sometimes it seemed to strike upon dead leaves, and then to hurry on again. This unseen march or progress was no echo of my own, for it kept an independent measure. The road was dull; twilight was closing in; the weather was dark and fitful; overhead the flying clouds were drifting across a lowering sky. All round about me the fogs and evening damps were rising. I thought of the warm fireside at Rock Villa I had left behind me; to be walking alone by this gloomy road was in itself depressing to spirits not very equable at the best of times, and this monotonous accompaniment jarred upon my nerves.

On one side of the road was a high hedge; on the
other, a rusty iron railing with a ploughed field beyond it. A little farther away stood a lodge by two
closed gates. The whole place had been long since
deserted and left to ruin—one streak in the sky
seemed to give light enough to show the forlornness
which a more friendly darkness might have hidden.
It is difficult to describe the peculiar impression of
desolation and abandonment this place produced
upon people passing along the high road. The
place was called "The Folly" by the neighbours,
and the story ran that long years ago some Scotch-
man had meant to build a palace there for his bride;
but the bride proved false; the man was ruined.
The house for which such elaborate plans had been
designed was never built, although the gates and
the lodge stood waiting for it year after year.

The lodge had been originally built upon some
fancy Italian model, but the terrace was falling in,
the pillars were cracked and weather-stained, the
closed gates were rust-eaten; the long railings, which
were meant to enclose gardens and pleasure-grounds,
were dropping unheeded. In the centre of the field,
a great heap showed the place where the founda-
tions of the house had been begun, and on the
mound stood a signpost, round which the mists were
gathering.

Meanwhile I hurried along, trying to reason away my superstitious fears. The steps were real steps, I told myself; perhaps there was some one behind the hedge to whose footsteps I was listening. I thought of the old Ingoldsby story of the little donkey and the frightened ghost-seer. I scolded myself, but in vain; a curious feeling of helplessness had overcome me. I could not even summon up courage to cross the road and look. I felt convinced that I should see nothing to account for the step which still haunted me, and I did not want to be thrown into terrified intangible speculations, which have always had only too great a reality for me. I was still in this confusion of mind, when I heard a sound of voices cheerfully breaking the silence and dispelling its suggestions, a roll of wheels, the cheerful patter of a pony's feet upon the road. . . . I turned in relief, and recognised the lamps of my aunt's little pony carriage coming up from the station. As it caught me up, I saw my aunt herself and a guest snugly tucked up beside her, with a portmanteau on the opposite seat.

The carriage stopped, to exclaim, to scold, to order me in. After a short delay the portmanteau was hauled up on the box to make room; Mr. Geraldine, the arriving guest, gave up his seat to me. I did not like to tell them how grateful I was for this opportune lift, or for the good company in which I found myself. The pony was not yet going at its full speed when we passed the lodge.

"Why, that place must be inhabited at last! there is a light in the window," said my Aunt Mary, leaning forward as we passed the lodge.

As she spoke, a figure came out to the closed gate, and stood looking through the bars at the carriage. It was that of a short, broad-set man, with a wide-awake slouched over his eyes, and a rough pea-jacket huddled across his shoulders. He seemed to be scanning the carriage; but when the lamps flashed in his face he drew back from the light. I just caught sight of a dull, sullen countenance; and as the carriage drove on, and I looked back, I saw that the solitary man was still staring after us, standing alone in the field where the streak of light was dying in the horizon, and the vapour rising from the ground.

"That is not a cheerful spot to choose for a residence," said Mr. Geraldine, deliberately. "What can induce anybody to live there?"

"Something, probably, which induces a great many people to do very strange things," said Aunt Mary, smiling: "poverty, Mr. Geraldine."

"That is an experience fortunately unknown to

me," said Mr. Geraldine, tucking the rug round his legs.

Rock Lodge is at some distance from a railway; the garden is not pierced by flying shrieks and throbs; it flowers silently amid outlying fields, with tall elm-trees to mark their boundaries. The road thither leads across flat country; it skirts a forest in one place, and passes more than one brick-baked village, with houses labelled, for the convenience of passers-by: Villa, Post Office, Schools, Surgery, and so on. We saw Dr. Evans's head peeping over his wire blind as we passed through Rockberry, and then five minutes more brought us to the gates of Rock Villa, where my aunt has lived for many years.

My cousins came out to greet the new comer. "Aunt Mary's bachelor," they used to call him in private; in public, he was "Uncle Charles." The two little boys, my aunt's grandsons, appeared from their nursery. There was a great deal of friendly exclaiming. The luggage was handed up and down. Little Dick seized Mr. Geraldine's travelling-bag, and nearly upset all its silver bottles on to the carpet. My aunt, Mrs. Rock, began introducing her old friend.

"You see, we have Nora and her boys, and Lucy and her husband," said she, cheerfully ushering him in, "and my niece Mary you know, and Miss Morier

I think you also know; she is in the drawing-room."
And then Mr. Geraldine was hospitably escorted into
a big room, with lights, and fire, and tea, and arm-
chairs, and conversation, and flowers, and a lady in
a shawl by the fire, and all the usual concomitants
of five o'clock.

II.

We had all been staying for some days at Rock
Villa, and enjoying the last roses of summer from
its warm chimney-corners. It is a comfortable, un-
pretending house standing in a pretty garden, which
somehow seems to make part of the living-rooms,
for there are many windows, and the parterres almost mingle with the chintzes; the drawing-room
opens into a conservatory; there is also a bow window with a cushioned seat, and a tall French glass
door leading into the garden. The conservatory di-
vides the drawing-room from the young ladies' room
or study, which again opens into the hall. The
dining-room is on the opposite side and the windows
face the entrance gates. Inside the house, as I have
said, the fires burnt bright in the pretty sitting-rooms;
outside, the glories of October were kindling in the
garden before winter came to put them all out. The
plants were still green and spreading luxuriantly,
stretching their long necks to the executioner; a
golden mint of fairy leaves lay thickly scattered on
the grass; from every branch the foliage still hung,

painting trees with russet and with amber. On the
stable wall a spray of Gloire de Dijon roses started
shell-like, pink against the sky. The guelder-rose
tree by the hall door was crimson, the chestnuts
were blazing gold.

The days passed very quietly; all the people in
the house were very intimately connected with one
another; married sisters are proverbially good company. The outside world was almost forgotten for
a time in family meetings and greetings and per-
sonalities; Nora's husband, the colonel, was in India;
Lucy's husband, the clergyman, came up and down
from London twice a week; Clarissa, the only unmarried daughter of the family, made music for us,
for Mr. Geraldine especially, who delighted in good
music; Miss Morier was also a very welcome visitor
in my aunt's house. For many years she had been
too ill and too poor to leave her own home; but her
health had improved of late, and a small inherit-
ance had enabled her to mix with her friends again.
She was a peculiar-looking woman, with dilating
eyes under marked brows; she may have been pretty
once, but illness had destroyed every trace of good
looks. She was very delicate still, and on her way
to the South for the winter; she was well educated,
well mannered, and full of ready sympathy; gold
and silver had she not in great abundance, but what

she had to bestow upon others was the case and
help of heart which real kindness and understanding
can always give. I could not help contrasting her
in my mind with Mr. Geraldine, who was also unmarried, and in his way full of friendly interest in
us all; but then it was in his way. He was easily
put out of it, easily vexed; punctual and, alas! often
kept waiting; he liked to lead the conversation, and
it rambled away from him; he was impatient of
bores and they made up to him; he didn't like ugly
people or invalids; he detested Miss Morier, and her
place was always by his at table.

Notwithstanding these peculiarities we are all
fond of him, and grateful too. Colonel Fox is supposed to owe his appointment to Mr. Geraldine's influence. Lucy's husband, the curate, declares that
half his parish is warmed and beflannelled with
Uncle Charles's Christmas cheque; there is no end
to his practical kindness and liberality. The intangible charities of life are less in our old friend's
way, perhaps. As we were all sitting round the fire
that evening after dinner, the conversation was turned
upon our meeting in the road.

"Were you frightened, Mary?" said my aunt;
"you were walking very fast."

"I was never more glad to see you, Aunt Mary,"

said I, gaining courage to speak of my alarm, and I told them my story.

"One has all sorts of curious impressions when one is alone," said my aunt, hastily. "You mustn't go out by yourself so late, my dear. It must have been fancy, for we should have seen any one following you."

"Footsteps?—how very curious!" said the curate. "Do you remember, Lucy, the other day I thought we were followed."

"Clarissa, will you play us something?" interrupted my aunt, rather uneasily; "and it is time for tea."

"You need not be afraid of my nerves," said Miss Morier, smiling. "I have quite got over my old troubles, dear Mrs. Rock, and I can hear people discuss hobgoblins of every sort with perfect equanimity."

My aunt evidently disliked the subject very much. She did not answer Miss Morier, and again said something about tea-time; but Nora, with some curiosity, exclaimed:—

"What was it, dear Miss Morier, that you used to see? I never liked to ask you; but I have always heard that you were troubled by some curious impressions."

"I don't mind telling you," said Miss Morier,

turning a little pale as if she had somewhat over-
rated her own strength of nerve. "I used to see the
figure of a man, a common-place looking man in a
wig, and muffled in some sort of cloak: you will
laugh, but you cannot imagine what misery it caused
me. At times I saw the whole figure advancing towards me; sometimes it was retreating; sometimes
only the head appeared. I found out at last that
by a strong effort of will I could dispel the phantom. When I was once convinced that it was some
effect upon my nerves brought on by physical weakness, I was able to overcome it. The apparition was
always accompanied by a peculiar sensation which I
can hardly describe; a sort of suspense and loss of
will, which came over me suddenly at all sorts of
times and in different places."

"I have been reading some of those accounts
of Shelley's visions, in that series of Morley's,"
said Mr. Geraldine, rather scornfully; "and the
mysterious attacks upon him, and the apparition
of the child coming out of the sea. He was a
vegetarian, and he only drank water, which more
than accounts for such cases of brain affection,"
said he, with a glance at poor Miss Morier, who was
a teetotaller.

"I can't agree with you in thinking it altogether physical," said the curate gravely. "If all

the tens of thousands of alleged phenomena witnessed in all parts of the world, and attested by experienced observers, be illusions, the fact would be more marvellous than the greatest marvel among them."

"But surely," said my aunt, impatiently, "the more common such things are, William, the more it also proves that it is a recognised affection depending on certain states of health not fully understood."

"All I can tell you," said I, "is that I heard the steps quite plainly." I spoke rather crossly, for they did not seem to give me credit for common sense. My aunt cut it short by saying I must not walk out alone again; and then came tea, music, bedroom candlesticks, good-nights. The curate went off with a pipe to some spot where tobacco was recognised at Rock Villa; Mr. Geraldine selected a book and a paper-cutter, and also disappeared; Clarissa, my youngest cousin, carried me off to her own room for a long midnight conversation. It lasted till the small hours, and I was creeping down to bed, carefully creaking through the sleeping house, when I thought I heard a faint cry. As I passed Miss Morier's door, I again heard it—a sort of agonised sigh.

I stopped short, and without further hesitation

opened the door, which was not locked, and walked
in. . . .

The room was full of moonlight; there was
no candle, only a dim nightlight burning near
the bed; the blinds were undrawn. In the middle
of the room stood Miss Morier, in her white dress-
ing-gown, with her long grey curls falling over her
shoulders. She looked very pale in the moonlight;
she gave a sort of gasp when she saw me.

"Who is it? What was it?" she said wildly.
"Have you also seen? Oh, tell me! Thank you
for coming." And then she caught me by the
arm, and burst out crying. "You will think me so
foolish," she sobbed, still clinging to me. "I thought
I was cured; my old trouble has come upon me
again to-night. I should not have talked of it. I
saw him there," she said, pointing to the window
and looking away.

I went to the window and saw nothing but the
broad moonlight upon the lawn and the shadows
of the bushes. There was a high clear frosty sky,
a few cold stars were shining above the trees, one
branch glistened and seemed to shake in the darkness.

Miss Morier recovered herself after a minute.
She drank some water, grew calmer, again thanked
me for coming, begged me to say nothing to any

one of her fright, and gratefully accepted my proposal that we should unlock the door between our rooms. Her alarm did not affect me, though I was very sorry for her, and after this night a certain slight barrier which had divided us hitherto seemed to be completely done away. I kept her secret as she desired. The subject was never mentioned between us. I could understand that the less she dwelt upon such nervous affections, the better it must be for herself and for every one else.

III.

But, perhaps, silence is not after all the best receipt for morbid impressions. I used to find myself watching Miss Morier, wondering whether her ghostly visitor was present to her; if she turned, if she looked about the room, as she had a way of doing, I used to imagine unseen visitants among us, or peeping over our shoulders. One day, in the garden, I thought I heard some one coming up to join me, and when I turned there was no one to be seen; then a curious uncomfortable sensation of being watched came over me, of something near and yet unrecognisable, of some one haunting my steps. One day Miss Morier came in from the fields and sat down impatiently by the fire. "Can you imagine what it is," she said, "never to be able to shake off the feeling of being followed? I never seem to be alone. I cannot bear it, I must get away. I think, perhaps, change of scene may help me."

I hardly knew how to answer her. This I knew, that I too had felt the same sensations. If we walked in the garden, there would be odd rustlings among the trees and bushes; sometimes of an evening it seemed to me that eyes were looking at us through the uncurtained windows; a sense of an invisible presence used to come over me suddenly as I sat busied with my own affairs; looking up, I might see nothing, but it would seem to me as if something had been there.

That very afternoon, after she left me, I remained alone in the drawing-room, reading by the fire and absorbed in my book, when this peculiar sensation of being watched made me turn round suddenly. This time I did see something which seemed to me more tangible than a ghost should be. It was a dark figure, starting from a corner of the room and vanishing into the conservatory. I saw it distinctly cross the window. I jumped up and followed, knocking over a table and a vase of flowers on my way; only, when I reached the conservatory, there was no one to be seen. The door was open to the garden and a chill wind was blowing in. Mr. Geraldine, hearing me call, came out from the study where he had been writing. I asked him if he had seen any one pass by, and he began some joking answer.

"It is no joking matter," I cried. "Pray do call some one."

We called everybody and looked everywhere, and searched the grounds, but nothing was discovered.

My younger cousins had also been in the study, and had seen nothing, heard nothing but the crash of the table. Mr. Geraldine continued his gibes, and I could see that the others only half believed me. The servants were desired to be careful about closing doors and windows. It was impossible to be really nervous in so large and cheerful a household, and by degrees the subject was dropped. Nevertheless, Miss Morier went on hurrying the preparations for her departure; she engaged a maid, packed her boxes; she was to start at the beginning of the week. She seemed in a fever to be off.

"Maria was always an excitable person," said my aunt, who was vexed by this sudden departure. "Once she gets a thing into her head, there is no changing her mind; she has always been fanciful since her trouble."

"What were her troubles?" said my cousin Nora. Then my aunt told us something of her friend's early life. She was to have been married to a young officer, who was killed in India, and she never really got over the shock, although she was once engaged to some one else. "It was her mother's doing, for the man was supposed to be rich; but it was a miserable business," said my aunt. "Maria nearly died of the strain. She seemed to hate the man, though he had obtained some strange power over her too. He was desperately in love with her, people blamed her for breaking it all off, but I always advised her to do so." My aunt ceased abruptly, for as she was speaking the door opened, and Miss Morier came in ready dressed for a walk.

"Is it prudent of you to go out?" said my aunt. "I don't trust these afternoon gleams."

"Oh, yes," cried Miss Morier, eagerly. "The day is fine, and I feel so well, and it is quite early yet." And then, as she seemed to wish for a companion, I offered to go with her.

We had paid our visit, and we were half-way home, when the fine sunshine suddenly vanished. It was gone, and then the clouds gathered overhead, and in a few minutes great chill drops began to fall in our faces. We had nearly half a mile to walk, and I felt not a little uneasy about my companion, who was very delicate, and not well able to bear sudden changes of temperature. We were walking along that straight high-road, of which I have already made mention, when the storm broke into a great downpour of rain and hail falling straight from the sky overhead. My companion was hurrying along by my side with flushed cheeks and panting

breath. We were very wet by the time we reached
the lodge, which looked more dismal than ever, pre-
senting its Italian columns to the rain; but some
shelter was to be found in the portico, and there we
waited till the violence of the rain should abate. It
was a dreary refuge enough; the field looked black,
and the mist was creeping along the ground, the
railings were dripping. It was early in the afternoon, but the evening seemed suddenly to be closing in. Maria Morier shivered and drew close to
the door, and then immediately we heard a creaking. The lodge door opened—two shaking hands
held it back for us.

"You can come in," said a voice; "the door is
open." Maria started, shrunk back, and then with
a strange fixed look, said faintly, "We must go in,
it is too late," and she walked into the lodge.

It consisted only of one room, big and dark and
dull, and scarcely furnished. There were two narrow
windows looking different ways, with lattice panes.
There was a big divan in a sort of recess. In the
centre of the place stood a round table with a velvet
table-cloth half pulled aside, and all stained and
dirty; the walls had once been papered with some
red flock paper, it was falling here and there in dis-
coloured strips. There was a medicine-bottle on
one of the window-ledges, with a pair of shabby old

boots covered with mud, and a candle stuck into a
bent and once gilt candlestick. As my eyes became more accustomed, I recognised the man I had
seen watching us through the gates. "You can wait
a bit," he said, but his voice frightened me, it was
so harsh and so hollow. His face looked pale and
sullen, but his eyes were burning. An old wig was
pulled over his forehead. He stood holding on by
the back of a chair.

———

IV.

The rain was still beating and pouring upon the roof and against the windows. The old man had sunk into the chair from which he must have risen to admit us; he sat staring at Maria with a curious watchful inquiring look. He put me in mind of some animal caged away and dazed by long confinement. A sort of mist came creeping from beneath the door. They both looked so strangely that I thought it best to try and speak, I could not understand their curious fixed looks.

"It is very kind of you to let us in," said I. "My friend is not strong, and might be seriously ill if we were out in the rain. It is very good of you to give us shelter."

"Shelter!" said the old man. "Don't you see that this is the gate-keeper's house—gates to nothing. I'm my own keeper."

He spoke with a sneer, and sank back with the effort. Then he began again, still staring at Maria Morier.

"I knew you were coming. You did not think

who it was that was about to give you shelter, or
you would have stood out drenching in the rain
sooner than come in."

He said all this a little wildly. I could not understand him. Miss Morier looked more and more
frightened, and I too began to be alarmed. We
had sat down upon the only convenient seat—the
divan in the recess. I took Maria's hand, it was icy
cold. The man sat fronting us, with his back to
the door. He did not speak like a gentleman, nor
as if he was a common man. Poor wretch! what a
miserable life he must have led for days past in this
lonely place. He began muttering to himself after
a while.

"'There she sits," I heard him say. "She is an
old woman now. Who says people change? I do,"
he shouted suddenly, starting to his feet; "they
change—they lie—they forget, d—— their false
hearts," and he dashed his hand to his head.

I was so startled by his sudden fury that I, too,
started to my feet, still holding my friend's hand.

"Does she look like a woman you might trust?"
he cried. "Smooth-spoken and bland, she fools us
all; poor fools and idiots, ruined for her sake. Ay,
ruined body and soul!"

By this time I was fairly terrified. Miss Morier,
strange to say, seemed less frightened than at first.

She looked at the door expressively, and we tried to get nearer to it; but he was too quick, and put himself in our way.

"*You* may go," he said, very excitedly, pointing to me. "I've taken you for her more than once, and nearly come upon you unawares, but to-day there is no mistake. I have waited for her all this time, and she can stay a bit now she has condescended to come to me. This might have been her lodge-gate once, all new and furnished up. It's not fit for my lady to bide in for an hour; but good enough for me to die in like a dog, alone."

It was a most miserable, terrifying scene. Miss Morier spoke very calmly, though I could see what a great effort she was making.

"I shall be glad to stay till the rain is over," she said; "and then, perhaps, you will show us the way back."

Her words, civil as they were, seemed to exasperate him.

"So you speak," he said, in a shrill sort of voice. "Mighty civil is my lady, but she shall not escape for all her silver tongue. I have followed you all these days,—followed your steps, waited your coming; and now you are come to me, and you shall not leave me, you shall not leave me!" he cried, in a sort of shriek, and I saw something gleam in his hand. He had got a knife, which he flourished wildly over her head. "Yes, you are come," he cried, "though you have forgotten the past, and David Fraser, the ruined man."

Miss Morier, who had been shaking like an aspen, suddenly forgot all her terror in her surprise and spontaneous sympathy. "*You* David! David Fraser! Oh! my poor David!" she said, stepping forward with the kindest, gentlest pity in her tones, and only thinking of him and his miserable condition, and forgetting all fears for herself.

I don't know whether it was her very kindness that overcame him. As she spoke, he threw up his arms and let them fall at his side, dropping the knife upon the floor. He seemed to catch for breath, and then, before we could either of us catch him, he had fallen gasping and choking at our feet. We could not raise him up, but Maria lifted his head on to her knee, while I loosened his shirt and looked about for water. There was no water, nothing in the place, and I could only soak my handkerchief on the wet flags outside, and lay it on his head. The rain was stopping; a boy was passing down the road, and I called to him, and urged him to hurry for help—to the doctor's first, and then to my aunt's house. I hastily wrote a pencil line upon the card for him to show, and he set off running. Then I went back into the house; it was absolutely bare, neither firing nor food could I find. There was a candle and there were some lucifers, which I struck, for the twilight was falling. "Some one will soon be here," I said to Miss Morier.

"Rub his hands," she said in a whisper; and we chafed the poor cold hands. The man presently came to himself, and began muttering again. As I looked at the poor patient, I could hardly believe this was the same man we had been so alarmed by. His wig had fallen off, and we could see the real lines of his head. He was deadly pale, but a very sweet expression had come into the sullen face. His talk went rambling on in some strange way. He seemed to know Miss Morier, for he kept calling her by her name. Then he appeared to imagine himself at some great feast or entertainment.

"Welcome to my house, Maria," he said; "welcome to the Towers. Tell the musicians to play louder; scatter flowers; bring more lights, it is dark; we want more lights."

As he spoke a curious bright reflection came shining through the window that looked towards the field.

"Is some one coming?" said Maria, trying to raise the helpless figure. "Oh, go to the door."

I went to the door and flung it open, and then

I stood transfixed. It was not the help we longed for. I cannot explain what I saw—I can only simply describe it. The light which had been shining through the window came from across the field: from a stately house standing among the mists, and with many lighted windows. I could see the doors, the casements all alight. I could even trace the shadows of the balconies, the architectural mouldings. The house was a great square house, with wings on either side, and a tall roof with decorated gables. There were weathercocks and ornaments, and many shining points and decorations. It seemed to me that, from time to time, some dreamy faint sound of music was in the air. It was all very cold; I shivered as I stood there, and all the while I heard the poor voice rambling on—calling to guests, to musicians. "Welcome to my house," he said, over and over again. "I built it for her, and she has come to live in it."

This may have lasted some minutes; then I heard Maria calling, and as I turned away suddenly the whole thing vanished. "Oh, come!" she said. Some gleam of recognition had dawned into the sick man's eyes. He looked up at her, smiled very peacefully, and fell back. "It is all over," she said, bursting into a flood of tears. A minute after, there came a knocking at the door—it was the doctor, but he was too late.

I cannot account for my story. I have told it as it occurred. When the doctor came, and I opened the door to him, the field was dark, the black shadows were creeping all about it, the signpost stood upon the mound.

I asked the doctor afterwards if he had seen anything coming along, but he said "No;" and when I told my story, he tried to persuade me it was some effect of the mists on the marshy ground; but it was something more than that. Perhaps a scientific name will be found some day for the strange influence of one mind upon another.

THE END.